Turning Tables

Turning Tables

LaVar Akins

ISBN: 099656540X
ISBN 13: 9780996565400
Library of Congress Control Number: 2015911134
LaVar Akins, Apopka, FL

Table of Contents

It All Happened So Fast

S he did not like this feeling of anxiety mixed with anticipation as her hands went from nervous and shaky to perspiring. Keisha had not dated much. She was a kind, generous
woman with a spiritual background and a big heart. However,
when she was on the dating scene, one of her no-no's was a man
with clammy hands; she hated when a man seemed unsure of
himself. She also had already prayed, so she was violating two
of her own rules. "If you are going to worry, don't pray, and if
you are already prayed up, then you ain't got nothing to worry
'bout, *glooo-ray.*" She could hear the sound of her mother's voice
in her head. However, there she sat in the doctor's office, waiting, shaking, and scared out of her mind. She had taken the test
at home; it was positive. Keisha also called her friend Tina and
asked her to buy a test; they watched the results together, and it
was also positive. Despite those test results, she was hoping that
the stress of her recent ordeal combined with the fact that it was
finals week caused her to have a false positive. If the tests were

wrong, she could continue to pursue her dreams in spite of the *colossal* mistake she had made. She was in the middle of the accident. *It all happened so fast* was all she could think. It seemed like just yesterday she stepped off a stage accepting a high-school diploma and almost minutes ago that she started her freshman year. However, that was well behind her.

This was her second year of college. She graduated from high school and left home to become a communications major at Florida Agricultural & Mechanical University (FAMU). She idolized Oprah Winfrey as a child and wanted to follow her dreams of becoming a television personality. Keisha was a member of the National Honor Society with a 4.4 grade point average, and was top ten in her class as she graduated high school with an associate's degree, being dually enrolled at the nearby community college. She was so disappointed because it was not supposed to be this way for her. Maybe for other loose girls, but she was focused and raised in the church; she knew better. She knew what she wanted out of life. Because she was considered a junior when she arrived at college due to her credit hours, Keisha had already begun her internship at the radio station in Tallahassee. She was not supposed to be like other students who majored in fun and minored in games.

"I am Keisha Nicole Moore, and that is what I will have out of life—more than what my humble beginnings afforded me." That was her common introduction to people, with a firm grip and a bright smile. That was what she strived for, more than the small country town offered and more than what her mother, Evelyn Moore, and grandfather, Michael Moore—whom she affectionately referred to as G poppa—could provide for her. She was supposed to make it out, make it big, and come back to take care of them. However, there she was in the doctor's office, waiting and perspiring, which turned to sweat and anxiety, which turned to certainty with the turn of a doorknob. *Urrruhhhnn.* As the door opened in a surreal fashion, everything seemed to move in slow motion and have a booming echoing effect. *TICK, TICK, TICK, TICK.* Every second on the clock became louder and more annoying—almost an isolated noise, as if it were the only thing in the room. She really did not hear much of anything but the loud, dramatic boom of the doctor's footsteps as he moved closer to her; she heard absolutely nothing after the doctor said, "Congratulations, Ms. Moore. You are going to be a mommy." *Mommy, mommy, mommy, mommy*—it echoed loudly as he began scribbling instructions and giving advice, but she did not get any of it. She was no longer in the moment, but caught in a flashback in her mind and just replayed how this all started.

Keisha showed up at FAMU ready for action in her second year. Tallahassee is not huge and it is somewhat slow paced. Once filled with clay roads, it has a rather country feel to the city. It is affectionately referred to as "The Hill." The capitol city of the state, where decisions made on Capitol Hill by lawmakers trickle down to the rest of Florida and it is a hilly place. Like most of Florida, the weather is slightly schizophrenic because it can go from cold and rainy to unbearably hot and humid in the same day. It is not a mecca for entertainment and not the destination for fun for most unless you are a college student. There are three schools in the city and to be in college, you realize that you are in the prime of your life, and independent surrounded by people your age many with a like mindset.

FAMU is one of the three schools and it is a Historically Black University. The HBCU experience is different for a few reasons. It is more of a family oriented experience. There is a shared bond at any university; a feeling of unity because of the love of the school. Well, at a HBCU, you have that and an additional bond. There is a connectedness based on the appreciation for the culture. A feeling that you are surrounded not just by the best and brightest of your generation but your family; and you root for them to do well. There is an appreciation for the diversity within the culture; there are so many eclectic personalities that every hue of the spectrum both literally and figuratively is represented. The beauty of the campus is always on display as history is blended with progressive movers and shakers. The future and the past culminate with the rich tradition of the school and the innovative trend-setting student of today. Most of the HBCUs are located in the southern states, but you can find students represented from almost every part of the world. FAMU is the quintessential HBCU, a model for all to follow. There are traditions that stretch back as far as the school, which started in 1887, and there is no shortage of culture and beauty. Once you hit The Hill, you instantly fall in love and you are instantly welcomed as family. FAMU is known for many educational reasons. The pharmaceutical program, colleges of engineering, sciences, technology and agriculture, the school of business and industry and several other programs receive notoriety; but it is also known as a place for fun for college students, there is a hype that surrounds FAMU.

The most notable part of the school is the band; it receives the most hype and has the greatest reputation, one that is well deserved and has been earned with years of excellence. The way the reputation has been earned is with work; no one organization puts as much time, effort, and energy into being great and the results are evident. The practices can be heard at several hours throughout the day and the members of the band are the best of the best. The band is often referred to as the Marching 100. It is impossible to cover all of the intricacies of exactly what goes on for someone who has never lived the experience, however it is easy to see for any casual observer that it is the highest level of performance that a band can achieve. The greatness that is frequently displayed appears effortless but it comes from great musicians that have put in countless hours of work and share a special bond that is unrivaled. Most often the band performs at halftime shows of football games where many travel just to watch them perform. However, the Marching 100 has played for too many prestigious events to attempt to name them all. FAMU is home to a great school and the greatest band and the band is the centerpiece of the entertainment when it is football season.

In Tallahassee and at FAMU especially, the city came alive during football season. There were so many things to do for young adults living in a college town from "Be Out Day" to the Kappa Luau or just tailgating outside of the stadium during a football game. While living in the dorm her first year, Keisha was never out of character. Like most colleges or universities, FAMU was a fun place if you made it fun. There were parties, social gatherings, outings to the mall, or "The Set" on Fridays, which was like a fashion show from 11:00 a.m. to at least 2:00 p.m. because of a pseudo–flea market vendor-style environment mixed with local and national celebrity sightings. However, Keisha was not one for the social scene; she would not be caught dead on The Set on a Friday, even though her dorm was literally in front of it. Despite her belief in eating healthy, she would forgo trips to the cafeteria just to avoid the commotion. She would leave her 8:00 a.m. class on Friday, make a run to the Orange Room for a snack, make a beeline to her dorm room, sleep her way through the day, and then get up and study after the foolishness had died down. However, that got old to Keisha *fast*. She would always have to listen to her roommate, Tina, talk about the great time she had at the skating rink, the football game, the club, or on a date. Keisha was not concerned at first because she was not completely an inexperienced hermit. She was by no measure unattractive; actually, she was quite the opposite. Keisha was a very beautiful, shapely country girl who dated throughout high school and lost her virginity right before she became a freshman at FAMU to her high-school sweetheart, Warren Bean, who was headed to the Navy. They decided that they would be friends and not attempt the long-distance thing because of their circumstances, figuring they would meet new people and did not want to pressure their relationship. However, she had known Warren all her life, and on her eighteenth birthday she gave her body to Warren as a present to herself because she knew they loved each other, and he would be sensitive and gentle. They developed a sexual relationship throughout that summer before he left for the service. She gained experience that summer after several encounters, but afterward, Keisha regretted sinning and decided to refocus her attention on education.

Although Keisha was driven, she was not immune to being a young adult, having to listen to Tina rave about her experiences with one guy in particular—he was *the man* on campus. He was the head drum major and a decorated musician; he was a radio personality on the campus radio station and quite the ladies' man.

Jarvis Alexander Williams—or, as he was known around campus and all of Tallahassee for that matter, JAWS—was not only a talented, accomplished percussionist but also a skilled trumpeter and clarinetist. He had a great appreciation for classical music but was always up on what was new. He was connected to many celebrities and entertainers because of his uncle, who was a very successful producer in the entertainment industry. However, Jarvis was not just a music geek; he was also an athlete. He was dominant in four sports in his high-school days and was offered scholarships in three of those—track, basketball, and baseball—at division-one schools; however, he turned them all down because he lived for one purpose: *the hundred*. Everything positive that Jarvis did was to bring excellence and light to the band. He absolutely loved the band; the tradition had been instilled in him as a child and it was not just something he did but it was who he was. He was the FAMU marching band. Many believed he literally bled orange-and-green music notes.

Tina would spend hours away from the dorm and come back with a story to tell and a glow on her face.

"Chyyyyyle, Keisha, let me tell you, I slept like a baby last night! Whoo!"

"Are you saying you woke up crying every four hours needing to be rocked and held?" Keisha sarcastically replied.

"Nope, I'm saying JAWS rocked me last night and put my lights out," Tina proudly proclaimed. "That man is God's gift to women. His touch is magical, and his stroke is perfection," she continued to boast.

"Um, *no!*" said Keisha. "Please do not bring God into this foolishness. And he is a gift, giving God knows what to every woman walking on this campus. All of you talk about him. You act like he yours! Do you know how foolish you sound claiming everybody's man?" She looked at Tina, who was confused, and waited for a response.

"He ain't mine, Keisha, not forever, but for last night he was. JAWS took a bite out of me, and I bit him back, because once JAWS locks on you, you are going to get lockjaw. The man is named after the fiercest shark to ever live, and everybody knows sharks are born swimming. We all know, and every woman who has ever dealt with him knows. So trust me, I get it: he does not belong to me. But, baby, it is a privilege just to go for a swim with the shark."

Keisha sighed and just continued typing away on her term paper as Tina cleaned. However, the stories about JAWS would not leave her mind. Keisha had never met or seen Jarvis Williams in person. She heard him on occasion while listening to the radio and saw him from a distance during halftime shows at the football games when Tina and the girls would drag her out of the dorm on the weekend. Still, she was so dedicated and persistent when it came to her academic pursuits that she just truly did not have the time to chase fantasies about men or put the effort into a relationship. She was ready to have fun and even considered dating Robert Clark, a coworker at 96.1, the major radio station in town where she was an intern. Robert was genuine and did not have the character of a man like JAWS. He was a recent graduate of FAMU, and he worked at the station full time. He was enamored with Keisha, frequently complimenting her. They would often do lunch together, sort of like miniature dates, but they were not officially in a relationship. Robert was the type of guy who could not find the right time to ask Keisha out despite being really fond of her, but was pleased with the way the relationship was progressing. He did not want to rush into anything. Keisha liked him, but she thought he had low goals. She wanted an ambitious man who could match her drive in life. Robert seemed too content to be working at the radio station. He talked about a career there, settling in Tallahassee. Keisha wanted much more out of life, so she never pushed for anything with Robert because she was fine with their relationship as it was.

One Tuesday morning early in her second year, Keisha had to go to Foote Hilyer, the administrative building for student affairs, to check on the status of her financial aid. She submitted paperwork the previous week and had been awaiting a response. She spent all day Monday winning the waiting game while on hold, playing phone tag with various counselors who were "aware of her issue and dealing with the problem." However, Keisha had heard that song and dance before, so she knew if she wanted her money in time, it would be necessary to stand in line all day until she sat in front of a decision maker. Someone who would push whatever buttons needed to be pushed or took her paper from the left side of the desk to the right side. She was frustrated with the process, but she had been through this two times before and realized it was like this for everybody, no exceptions. If you want your money, then you better go and see about it; that was just the way it was. Well, Keisha packed a snack, prepared for hours of waiting, and hiked it from the dorm room. Over the hills she went, with her backpack, some reading material, and a positive mind-set. The weather was nice that morning, just a very beautiful day. As she entered Foote Hilyer, there was an odd vibe about the building—in fact, to that morning in general; everything seemed very peaceful, almost like the calm before a hurricane. When she entered the financial-aid line, she was shocked to notice something very peculiar: there was no real line. There were only five people. Keisha was dumbfounded, so she tapped the guy in front of her and asked, "Hey, are they about to close early, or is something wrong?"

He chuckled and said in a familiar voice without really turning around, "I thought the same thing; maybe the computers were down or something. But no, it is just odd; there's no one here today!"

"Thank you, Jesus," she quietly exclaimed. She thought about it as she continued mumbling to herself. "Now, this is favor. I knew there was an air to the building today. Look at God shifting the atmosphere, just turning it around for me, didn't he do it?"

Despite there not being many people in line, financial aid is financial aid. No one issue can be handled quickly and none of the people who are "helping" you are fast. She stood there almost an hour and thirty minutes as she began humming one of her favorite songs so she would not get frustrated. It was the song she sang in church on third Sundays, her G poppa's favorite song. While humming, she remembered the paper that she needed was in her bag, so she knelt down to get it out, figuring now was the time to get it because she was about third from the window. A strange thing happened, though, while she was retrieving the form from her bag: Keisha stopped humming, but the song did not stop.

The guy whom she tapped earlier kept singing. "I said I feel like holding on!" he sang unashamedly. She looked and her eyes popped out. As he turned around toward her, he said, "I apologize, but that is just one of my favorite parts of the song.

You sounded so peaceful earlier it was calming my spirit. I get a little nervous and frustrated when I'm in here waiting in line. I did not want to interrupt, but my granddaddy, God rest his soul, used to love that song, and I would play the piano in church when my cousin would sing it."

"It is no problem at all. You have such a beautiful voice. Do you sing?" Keisha asked him.

He retorted, "No, I give instructions, and I correct mistakes with the sound of my voice, but my singing days ended at about twelve at Jackson Temple Missionary Baptist Church. Played the drums from then on and I have not really been a singer since then."

"Oh really? That is such a travesty. You sound so nice," she stated, as she began to look at him really for the first time, noticing just how attractive he was. He stood about six foot three and was country strapped—just muscular for no reason. He had deep dimples and looked like a human candy bar, the most beautiful shade of chocolate. She began to get lost in his eyes. He was not really well dressed but still looked up to date, in a tank top and khaki shorts obviously to display his physique. There was a confidence to him that was just enough—not cocky, but comforting. He smelled nice, was well groomed, and conversed with her for more than two seconds without referring to sex. She became overwhelmed and introduced herself as she fumbled over her papers. "Well, well, well, hi, I-I am Keisha Moore." She stuttered as she extended her hand.

He gripped hers firmly, but not too roughly, as he gently said, "My name is Jarvis. It is a pleasure to meet you, Keisha." As they shook hands, Keisha could barely hear him because the bellowing sound of *"Neeeext!"* was the only thing that could be heard. Jarvis stepped to his window. Immediately, Keisha followed to the window next to Jarvis as she heard; "I can assist the next person." He was helped quickly, and miraculously, so was Keisha. She was out of the line before Jarvis in two minutes with a printed letter stating that she would receive her net check in three days, just in the right amount of time. Keisha pretended to organize her things in her bag before she left, needing a reason to hang around and wait on Jarvis as she looked him over again. He walked toward her and said, "I can't believe it. They are never this efficient."

"I know, right? Who you tellin'? This is clearly like the best day ever. What other songs do you like, if you don't mind me asking?" Keisha inquired as they began walking.

"Well, I love all music, and I am all across the board with all music genres. I love every song from Tupac; however, my all-time favorite song is 'The Reason Why We Sing.' That song is just incredible to me, and I absolutely love 'Open Up My Heart.' Now, that is my jam," Jarvis told Keisha.

"I know this is awkward, but I was about to grab breakfast off campus. Would you like to go with me?" Keisha asked.

"There is nothing awkward about it. I'm rolling with you. I love food and great conversation. If you do not mind me saying so, you are absolutely stunning, so I would go anywhere with you." Jarvis was smooth with all of his responses; nothing seemed sexual. He was just confident, and that seized Keisha's attention.

They walked towards Keisha's car and spotted Soul Train loading up his cooler with drinks and snacks. He was talking to a group of students about the time he spent with royalty, showing them pictures, and telling them about his cars. They could overhear him telling the students that they should travel the world to experience different cultures as they passed by. Keisha had a close parking space, so they got into her car and rode to a nearby fast-food place, where they got a quick bite to eat as they started to get to know each other.

"Where were you headed? Do you live on campus?" Keisha asked.

"No, actually, I have an apartment not far from here. You can drop me off there, if it's not a problem."

Jarvis asked Keisha to tell him more about her. She opened up and did not stop talking as he gave her directions to his apartment. As they pulled in, Keisha felt embarrassed that she had rambled for the duration of the drive, never giving Jarvis the chance to talk. Because she monopolized the entire conversation, she did not know much about him.

She looked at him and said, "I'm *so* sorry, but I wanted to get to know you. I am running my big mouth and did not really ask you anything."

"Are you kidding? I love listening to you. You have a relaxed, calming voice that places me at ease. However, you are assertive, and you enunciate properly, not to mention that you are disciplined, determined, and ambitious. Your look is unique because of your hazel eyes and natural, flowing hair. I believe that is going to be a great look not just for you, but also for our people on major network television. I honestly do not think there is anything that you cannot accomplish. Really, I could listen to you all day." Again, Jarvis was always smooth. He was being genuine. Nothing Jarvis said to Keisha was a line; he just had no problem being himself. His natural appreciation for women was what made him a lady-killer.

Keisha heard Jarvis say that she could talk all day and almost had an "eargasm"; that was the most arousing thing she had ever heard. She loved to talk, and Jarvis was actually listening to her sincerely, hanging on to her every word, and made an inference about something she mentioned in conversation. This type of authenticity was rare in life; she had not found it at all in college, especially not with any man. All the boys she met in college talked about sex almost as an introduction, but this guy had not mentioned it, and they were together for almost an hour. Her mind was blown.

Jarvis told Keisha, "Well, my roommate is out of town, and I have to clean the place. It is an absolute mess, and I have to run to the grocery store. We can exchange information, and I could catch up with you to talk or hang out later if you want."

As they exchanged numbers, Keisha looked and said, "You can put your stuff down in your place while I finish my burger, and I will take you to the store."

"OK, I'll be right back," Jarvis said.

Keisha began talking to herself as she finished her food. "Well, the whole day cannot be perfect. I wanted pancakes, but they always stop serving breakfast as soon as I pull in line; it never fails. At least I am meeting a good guy and getting my net check on Friday. I can finally go shopping this weekend and snag those boots I have been wanting. I got to let him talk when he gets back in this car. I don't know anything about him. I could not even hear his name plus I can't tell how old he is." She scarfed down her food then began sipping her drink as Jarvis returned. She said, "OK, this time I want to listen, tell me about you."

He started as she drove down the busy street. "OK. Again, my name is Jarvis Williams, and as you know, I love music. I am

also very passionate about our children becoming more edu-
cated, so I am a senior music major with a minor in elementary
education. I *am the band, and it is me!* Everything I do is for my
love of the school and the band."

SKUUURRRRD! Keisha slammed on her brakes and pulled to
the side of the road as horns honked from cars swerving to avoid
accidents. "Holy fudge cake; shut the front door! You are JAWS?!?"

Jarvis looked as puzzled as he could possibly be because he
thought she knew. He recovered, though, because she clearly
had a problem with him, but he was ignorant as to why. Was she
a scorned ex-lover, the friend of one, or what? "No, I am Jarvis
Alexander Williams. I will be JAWS when I take the field on
Saturday, on the radio later this week, and with the kids later today. But right now, I'm just Jarvis. If you have a problem with
that, I will get out and walk, because I love myself and the Lord,
but I don't know if I want to meet him today, not like this," he
explained calmly, attempting to settle Keisha down. "Would you
like me to get out of your car?" Jarvis politely asked Keisha as he
began gripping the door handle to open it.

"I don't think that is necessary. I apologize. You—you just
seemed so nice and respectful and decent and so…well, I don't
know." Keisha blundered over her words as she was completely
blindsided. There was no way in the world that this man was the
same creep who ruined the campus.

"Well, clearly, you have let the rumors define me. Do not let
me offend you by actually getting to know you or allowing you
to know the real me, and honestly, I don't do drama or crazy
situations. It really is not a problem. I am getting out. I can get
back home. Really, it was nice to meet you." He began attempting to exit the vehicle again.

She locked the doors and said, "No, really, I'm sorry. I'll drive you."

He looked at her and said, "Woman, let me out of this car!"

Keisha just laughed and drove toward the grocery store. There was an awkward silence for the first time in their interaction so Keisha turned up the radio until she dropped him off at the store. She tried to rescue the moment with a joke.

"You want me to wait, or are you scared to get back in?"

Jarvis looked back in the window of the car when he exited and asked, "Hell, should I be? I really don't know."

They both smiled, and she told him, "Hurry back, boy!"

Keisha franticly waited in the car. "I cannot believe that this is actually JAWS. I should call Tina and tell her about this foolishness." Keisha continued to talk to herself as she dialed her friend. "Dang, no answer!" She waited for the voice mail. "Gurrrrl, Tina, you are not going to believe this. You will not believe who I met in Foote Hilyer today, girl. Call me right back when you get this, Tina. I mean right, right back! Bye."

Keisha's mind continued to race as she sat in the car whispering nervously as if she was in a conversation with someone else. "What if he really is just a nice guy? I mean, he has been so polite and respectful. He listens so well, and he knows so much about church. Yeah, see, that is important, church. He has those muscles, too; man, he got them *muscles*, though, plus he is all chocolate and stuff. But I am no clown; I mean, he does this with everybody, right? And me, I can't go for that. I'm a good girl. I gave this fool my real phone number. I usually only give guys my e-mail or fakes. I can't be caught up with this stupidity. Maybe I can change him." She looked over at some of his belongings that he left behind in the car, grabbed the slip of paper with her number on it, crumpled it up, threw it out the window of the car, and watched it roll into the drain.

As she persisted with thoughts about Jarvis, he opened the door, back with his cleaning supplies in his hand. "I decided to be brave and return." Jarvis kidded to see where her demeanor was.

"Well, honestly, I'm glad that you did. I won't chicken out either," Keisha told him.

"Look, I am going to be honest with you, Keisha. I have a past. Truthfully, I have a present, but I'm all man. I love women. I'm not an absolute saint. I am, however, a work in progress. I'm not as bad a guy as you may have heard. I have never—and I mean never—forced anyone to do anything. I try to treat people with class and respect. My momma taught me that, and I have her to thank for so much. I understand if you have heard some things about me, and I respect it if that makes you not want to be my friend. I have been lied on before however I earned most of the reputation some people put on me, because I have done a lot here in Tallahassee," Jarvis said in a sincere tone to make an effort to lay it all out in the open.

"Jarvis, no one is perfect. We all get grace and mercy. Lord knows I have received it, or I would not be here today. I am going to accept you for the person that you are—the one I am meeting today. I mean, I have nothing to forgive you for and no reason to hate you. All of your whore records are yours, and I am sure you are proud of them." She began to laugh as she threw the joke in at the end to bring some fun back in the conversation.

"Oh, so you doing it like that. You just going to throw that in there at the end, huh? Good shot, but I'm Teflon. So I tell you what, Mrs. All Your Whore Ma Muh Ma Muh," Jarvis mocked Keisha.

"What?" Keisha asked.

"I'm rubber. You're glue. Whatever you say bounces off me and sticks to you," Jarvis teased.

"That sounds mature, very good little boy." Forever-cynical Keisha never missed an opportunity to be sarcastic as she patted his head.

They returned to the apartment without incident. Jarvis exited with the bags in his hands and said to Keisha, "You are really cool. I enjoyed hanging with you this morning. See you around."

"Oh, so you are not going to invite me in?" Keisha asked, as she looked upset while rolling her eyes at him with her neck cocked halfway to the side.

"You can come help me clean if you want. I have to go to the hospital later, so I need all the help I can get because I only got three hours before my appearance."

Keisha came in and flopped down on the couch, pretending not to help. Jarvis tossed a rag at her. She threw it back to him playfully and told him, "I am not interested in cleaning this whore sty," but she helped anyway. They played music as they worked while Keisha talked, which is her favorite thing to do. Jarvis listened because he was getting help and he was seriously into Keisha. Her energy was just different to him, nothing like anything he had ever experienced. They finished up around 1:30 p.m. Jarvis looked at Keisha, gave her a church hug, and said, "Thank you, Sister Moore."

Keisha was almost offended. She could not believe that he had not tried anything with her. She had heard so much about this ruthless assassin. She began to ask herself questions in her mind: *I wonder if he thinks I'm ugly? He said I was stunning earlier. Why didn't he attack me? Does he not want me? Why not? I know he wants this!*

Her curiosity began to get the best of her, so she asked, "So, are you going to answer if I call you later because I am about to go?"

"Of course I will. I mean, for the next two hours I'll be working with the kids. So you can call any time after that. Oddly enough, I don't have any practices today; usually, I'm at practice all week especially when we have home games. I'm headed to the hospital. You can come along if you want or just hit me up afterward," responded Jarvis.

"I was planning on living in financial aid today, so I ain't got much to do. I love to be a blessing to somebody else, especially a kid," Keisha said.

"OK, I'll be out in a minute. I'm going to jump in the shower. The remote is over there," Jarvis told her as he pointed to the gadget.

Oh, OK. I get it now, Keisha thought. *This is his move. He is going to ask me to shower with him, or he is going to come out with the water all over his fresh, clean body. I knew I was not ugly. I will sit here and play along with this fool, because he ain't getting none of this, not today.* Keisha sat and waited as she lowered the volume on the television, curiously listening for a change in the water while expecting Jarvis to sneak out and try something.

About twenty minutes later, she noticed Jarvis coming from his bedroom fully clothed in nice attire. He was wearing a suit and tie, looking as professional as anyone she had ever seen.

Keisha snatched her purse and keys. Jarvis said to her, "Well, gorgeous, if you will ride with me, I'll drive this time, because you have been nice enough to chauffeur me around all morning. Plus, I ain't no punk or nothing, but I am afraid you may stop in the middle of traffic, and I do not want to end up stretched out all on Madison Street." Jarvis extended his hand to Keisha to help her off the couch.

"I may not stop the next time. I may just leave you, as soon as we get to Madison," she said to him playfully. "See how you deal with that."

They rode to the hospital. Jarvis gave an inspirational speech to the children about chasing their dreams and him living his. He was in such control of the crowd that she was impressed with how focused the audience was; they were pin-drop silent. He even took the time to introduce her to the kids, told them that she was going to be a star, and that they should remember her name. He interacted with the kids after a question-and-answer session. They were very engaged; hands shot up in the air when it was time to ask something, because the kids were attentive as he spoke. Before he closed, he gave away some posters, T-shirts, and band paraphernalia. He truly enjoyed himself while he was there. Keisha surprisingly did as well as she played with the kids. She had never heard of this side of JAWS. He was just a regular person to her—charismatic and very attractive. He was even intelligent in his own way and driven by his desire of children, education, and music.

On the way home, they stopped to get food at a place near Tennessee Street and High Road. They grabbed two boxes of chicken fingers with the most addictive sauce known to humans. Jarvis was a star; the drum majors at historically black universities are like the quarterback of the football team at other schools. The people in the restaurant knew him and were glad to serve him. It was beyond any normal popularity. Nevertheless, to him, it was all about one thing: bringing prestige and pride to the name of the band.

He was a part of a great legacy of musicians and he reiterated constantly, "I just want to give the people something to believe in. A sound that represents us as a people, something they can use as a soundtrack to life and be proud of. *I live for this!*"

It was a joy to see him living in his purpose, which was the way Keisha came to view Jarvis—just as a delightful human being who was living life fully and enjoying every minute of it. It was really too late for her; she was fully entangled and there was no stopping her at this point. Jarvis pulled into his apartment complex, hopped out of his car, and walked around the back of the car to open the door for Keisha. However, she was already out of the car, heading toward the apartment.

"Last one to the door is a rotten egg." Keisha laughed as she sprinted toward the door. Jarvis chased her as they got to the door simultaneously, but Jarvis tapped the door and said, "I win." Keisha was completely out of breath at this point as she uttered, "Yeah, but I ain't drop none of this chicken, though," in between deep breaths and gasps for air.

They laughed. Jarvis opened the door. He said, "You can chill out here and finish up with the food. You know where the remote is. I cannot wait to get out of this suit!" He began heading back toward his room.

By the time he got to his bedroom door, he felt weird as the hairs on the back of his neck rose; he was being followed. "Let me help you with that. I can't wait to get you out of that suit!" Keisha whispered to Jarvis as he tripped over his feet while turning around. She began kissing his lips slowly as she took off his jacket. Jarvis fell back first on the bed, as Keisha pulled up her sundress and straddled him. She ripped the buttons from his

shirt and continued kissing, rubbing his chest and grinding ag-
gressively against his pants.

The tables had turned. She felt he was vulnerable and took advantage of him. It was time he turned around the situation. Jarvis
was somewhat stunned, caught off guard but he always taught to
stay ready. He usually noticed blood in the water, but at this point,
he had not even begun to think of sex with her. He knew he would
not disappoint. He kissed her back and grabbed her hair as she
moaned. He began caressing her back, as she grew hotter. Keisha
was soaking through her panties, as Jarvis cuffed a handful of her
round cheeks still unable to grip it all. He flipped her over. They
kissed even more. Jarvis had a reputation, and it needed to be up-
held. He backed away from the bed, took off the rest of his clothes,
and watched her reaction. Mesmerized by what she saw; this man
was every bit the gladiator that he had been described as his body
was almost as impressive as his package. Keisha bit her finger and
waited, wondering if she could take all of him. She moaned even
louder as she began to rub on her body with her moistened fingers. He began to undress her in his mind before he touched her
again. As he strutted toward her, he wanted to make sure she knew
this was special to him. He took her by the hand, pulled her from
the bed, and kissed her with desire. She melted. He began removing her clothes with anticipation while kissing her sensually all
over. He pulled her sundress over her head. Jarvis appreciated
every curve on Keisha's body. Once he got to her underwear, he
effortlessly unhooked her bra and pushed her roughly on the bed.
Playfully starting with his teeth, he slid her panties off. Once she
was completely bare, he stopped to admire her canvas. He whispered in her ear, "I have never seen a more beautiful sight in my
life" as he began to make love to her.

He kissed her luscious, rose petal soft lips and made his way to her neck, alternating between kissing and licking, the flick of his tongue almost made her erupt. He gently rubbed her as he continued moving down her body; he took his time at her breast, sucking her nipples with passion. Keisha was boiling at this point. He came up and kissed her more. Keisha was almost angry because she was so ready to feel him inside of her. Jarvis then repositioned his body as he slid down the bed, while pushing her closer to the headboard. He wrapped his arms around her legs. Starting at her belly button, he continued going down gliding his tongue and separating her legs further. He kissed her inner thighs then slightly turning his head to her lips. Keisha could not take it anymore she screamed as the pleasure overwhelmed her. Jarvis had a magical tongue and he knew exactly what to do with it. Jarvis began to get erect as he continued to please Keisha. Keisha's thighs became like earmuffs on Jarvis the more the pleasure intensified. She tightly gripped the back of his head almost to guide him, despite him not needing any help. Her moans were like a road map to her body that drove him to her hot spots. He started moving his knees forward and entered her as they exchanged grunts and groans settling into a groove. Keisha was discovering that not all the talk about Jarvis was hype, it actually did not do him justice; he was a technician in the bedroom. Once he finished fully appreciating her body with a sensual type of love making that one would usually reserve only for a first-love, he began to rigorously pound away on her. He beat her like a bass drum, as she screamed no longer able to contain any of what she was feeling; the sensation was mind-blowing. She climaxed quickly, almost embarrassingly, but he did not make her feel uncomfortable. Laying at ease, she rested in his arms a moment and began kissing him again. This went on for about two hours. As they worked their way around the apartment, moving from the wall, to the floor, to the counter, to the sofa, eventually ending up back in the bedroom, she slipped into ecstasy. Keisha fell asleep in a puddle of lust and infatuation. She was exhausted and drained, but bewilderingly, she did not feel bad. She felt no shame; she just felt pleased.

She woke up early in the morning, feeling around in the bed. *OK, where are you, Kee Kee?* She thought as she began to try to get her bearings. *What time is it, and where in the world am I? OK, phew! I'm dreaming; for a minute there I thought I slept with JAWS. Just go back to bed, girl,* she continued thinking as she felt around the bed again and realized she was alone. Then she thought about it some more. *Hold up. I'm not dreaming! This ain't my bed. I did sleep with him. I am alone. This dirty dog left me. He left me in his apartment and did not have the decency to even say bye. I could tear this whole place up. I can't believe I have been this stupid,* she thought. Finally, she made a sound when she let out a scream. "Ughhh!"

Jarvis rushed in wearing only an apron. "Are you OK?"

"Oh, oh yeah, I'm fine. I didn't realize, I mean, I thought you had, uh, I just didn't think you were still here." Keisha was never this bumbled in her speech, but everything Jarvis did left her dazed.

"Well, I sort of live here, and it is very early in the morning. I couldn't sleep, so much was running through my mind, so I decided to get up and cook you breakfast. You seemed upset yesterday when we didn't get through the fast-food line in time and that always happens to me. So I whipped you up something. I'm out of orange juice. I started to go to the store and get some, but I didn't want to leave you here in unfamiliar territory by yourself." Jarvis remained smooth.

Keisha sniffed, and sure enough, the aroma of eggs and sausage filled the air. She had no idea he would be this sensitive and caring. She looked around the room, gathered her clothes, and began to get dressed. She followed Jarvis into the kitchen as she checked her cell phone. She noticed that she had four missed calls and one voice-mail message from the previous night. The voice mail was from Tina. She listened to it: "Hey, Keish, sorry I missed your call, girl, but I was at work busy out of my mind, chyle. I'm so anxious to hear about who you met. It was probably Shirley Ceaser, Kirk Franklin, or somebody the way you was all amped up on the phone, girl. Now that I'm off, though, me and the girls going up to twenty-five-cent wing Tuesday and hangout with the football players. It will take me a while to get jazzy, so call me back if you want to go, and I'll come get you. If I do not hear back from you, I will just get you some wings. Love you to pieces. Call me back, boo."

Keisha looked at Jarvis and could not believe she found herself in this predicament. Again, her thoughts were all over the place. On the one hand, she was pleased she had met somebody new, somebody nice, and seemingly genuine. However, she was no hypocrite; she told anybody who would listen that this man was no good. She was beyond nervous, almost shaky. Jarvis set down a glass of water beside Keisha as she was eating at the table. Keisha thanked him for the food, then clumsily spilled the water on top of her things and ruined some papers as a result. Water was everywhere. The slip of paper she had written Jarvis's phone number on got drenched, making it impossible to read.

He rapidly grabbed a paper towel to wipe up the water. "Don't worry about any of that. I'll take care of it. Do you need to keep any of this?" Keisha shook her head no. Jarvis threw the papers away, cleaning up the mess while being super attentive to Keisha. He never felt like this before today. Keisha finished most of her breakfast. She drank what was left of the water as she hurried to gather her things.

"Look, Jarvis, I got to get to class. I had a really nice time with you and all, but I—I…" She did not really know how to leave. The shame was triumphant at this point. Her mind was still sprinting with conflicting thoughts.

Jarvis interrupted, "Please do not worry your pretty little head. I understand. I'll give you a call later today. Your number is in my portfolio. I do not go anywhere without that thing. I want to give you something." After he hugged her, he handed her a note that he had written while he was cooking breakfast.

Keisha rushed to her car, said a brief prayer, and then opened the note before she started the ignition.

The world is yours. Go get all you deserve, a beautiful mind and a body with the perfect curves. Your skin looks like it has been kissed by the sun with the perfect amount of melanin. Beautiful black queen, I believe you will make me better than I have ever been. Your elegance is only matched by your intelligence. Keisha, I want more of you because I believe you are heaven sent.

It was somewhat corny but sweet. As she thought about it, there was a certainty in her mind: he did this with everybody. This was all a game to him, and she had been played. She could not believe that she had defiled her body being like some of these other silly women. She was better than that. Keisha got to campus, rushed to her room, brushed her teeth, showered, and then ran to her class arriving about two minutes late. Usually, she was front and center eager to participate, but that day, she sat quietly in the back. Feeling an aura of guilt as if people could see it or as if an odor of shame just permeated her surroundings, she did not want to be seen. As her class ended, she gathered her things and walked briskly back to her room and fell asleep.

When she woke up, Tina was in their room. Tina looked at Keisha and started in. "Hey, girl, I had been calling you back. Now I see why you ain't answer; you in here *knocked out!* That is that real sleep; I am talking about that *sleep* sleep. Like you been put down. I know; I been there before."

"I don't know what you are talking about. I just took a little nap after my morning class," Keisha responded as she tried to get up, still feeling somewhat groggy.

"A little nap, tsshuh! Your morning class is still an eight o'clock class, right? Well, your 'little nap' got you getting up at six o'clock in the evening, girl," Tina explained with an attitude.

Keisha looked at the clock. It was 6:12 p.m. She'd slept right through the day. This was not like her. She was up to date on all of her assignments and did not have to go in to work for two days. She had not really missed anything, but still, she did not like the way she had been acting.

"Your momma called. She wants you to call her right back, and I promised her you would. The last thing I want is Momma Moore mad with me. She may not cook for me anymore, so please call her back," Tina joked.

Keisha, still sleepy, picked up the phone and dialed home "hey, Momma."

"Hi, baby, you been on my heart heavy the last two days. Is everything OK?"

"Yes, ma'am, why would you ask that? On your heart how?"

"I don't know, but your G poppa came in from the front porch and said he had a feeling in his spirit about you. So I called and didn't get an answer yesterday or this morning. I was worried until Tina told me you were sleeping. I was 'bout to gas up Pearl and get to getting. Your G poppa said he was going to grab his gun out of the drawer upstairs and ride with me. You eating right up there, ain't ya, baby? Did you eat breakfast this morning?"

"Yes, ma'am, I had sausage and eggs; and don't nobody won't you on the road with that big white pickup truck knowing that it probably won't make it."

"Well, that's good, baby. I was worried, but I know you got it under control. I'm late for choir practice, but I wanted to make sure I talked with you before I headed down to the church. I'll talk to you later, baby. I love you."

"I love you, too, Momma!"

Then they both said, "I love you Moore," as they hung up, it was their family thing.

Tina was staring at Keisha when she got off the phone. "Um, I ate in the café this morning, and they had grits and bacon; so where does this sausage and eggs come from? Are you lying to Mrs. Evelyn?"

"No, touch your nose, and why are you all in my Kool-Aid? Please get you some business!"

"Whatever. Seriously, though, I wanted to know why you were so hyped yesterday. I tried to call you back a few times and could not get you. Who did you see in financial aid?"

"Girl, I don't really remember much. I was just happy because I got my notice that my net check was coming." Keisha did not like lying, but she was too embarrassed to come clean at this point.

As time went by, things returned to normal. She decided to go to the football game with her friends and was happy when she saw Jarvis during halftime. She heard girls screaming hysterically for JAWS as he and the other drum majors gyrated sexually to the latest songs. She was immune to the screaming and was over the ordeal—not completely, but enough to be composed in the moment. It happened, but it was over. She was definitely not much for one-night stands for any woman, especially not herself, and would take this secret to her grave. Nevertheless, she healed, and aside from some of the guilt, she was almost delighted it happened. Keisha and her friends decided to come back to the dorm room after the game, skipping the parties and the nightclub scene to relax for the night. Shakela, Tina, Keisha, and Lynnesia were all in the room watching a movie. Lynnesia was the girlfriend of Morris Bright. Morris and Jarvis were close friends and roommates. Shakela and Tina were friends of Jarvis; Tina had previously been intimate with Jarvis and had an ongoing kind of off-and-on sexual relationship with him. They had more of a friendship that developed because Tina had started seeing a new guy and stopped reaching out to Jarvis. Shakela and Jarvis met recently and developed a quick fling. As they all sat in the room eating popcorn, a love scene appeared in the film.

Tina looked at Shakela as she shouted, "I know who that reminds me of, girl. He is putting it down!"

"Yeah, but he been tripping lately. I could not get him to hang out all week. I have only known him for about a month now, but he called me back and told me he was going to be busy. That this week was not a good time because they are heading on a trip to Atlanta, so he would not have much time now or for the rest of the semester. I almost cussed him out, but I know he will be changing his tune after homecoming. So I was like, OK, whatever," Shakela admitted.

"He in love, y'all," Lynnesia chimed in.

"Who?" all three girls responded in unison as they eagerly looked at Lynnesia.

"What you mean, *who?* I know it sounds crazy, but I was right there on Mo's lap when this boy JAWS floats in the house just whistling. Mo asked him, 'What's up with you, clown? What got you feeling so good?' And I mean, this boy was downright skipping around the house at this point. He looked at my baby and me and said, 'I have been struck by an angel.' We looked at each other and busted out laughing. But he did not stop there. He said he really likes this girl, that he can't find her number, but he ain't doing nothing with nobody until she calls him back. That boy usually don't go two days without at least a few women coming through that apartment." Lynnesia made it clear to the rest of the girls.

"Love? Not JAWS. Ain't no love," Tina responded.

"You tripping, Lynn! JAWS will let you know up front that you are not the only one and that he does not do drama. So why would he lock in with one girl when half of Tallahassee is throwing panties at that boy, and the other half is waiting in line to throw they panties at him?" Shakela asked, appearing puzzled while waiting for a response.

"Well, not everybody is waiting in line, Kela. Sister-do-right over here, Keisha Moore, thinks he is the devil himself and has single-handedly ruined the campus." Tina giggled at her own comments.

"Well, I will tell you this. You know JAWS and me usually go at it because he says I am at the house too much. That fool used to call me 'Lynn the loveseat.' He likes to say I am in their living room more than the sofa, always clowning, asking how much I got on the light bill or telling me he is going to need my part of the rent. Lately though, he has never been more pleasant to be around, been singing around the house and all. He has been extra nice to me. Before they packed for the trip to the classic against State, he told me if I could not reach Morris not to worry, because he was going to make sure he would keep an eye out. You know they left tonight right after the game. This clown dedicated a gospel song to the girl on his show the last two days and he swears he is a changed man. He wrote her poetry, like a little rap or something, and cooked her breakfast the next morning after they hung out, according to Mo. He will not say if they had sex or not, and he has only been answering to Jarvis—won't even respond to JAWS. Mo thought I wasn't listening when he asked Jarvis what the booty was like. Jarvis told him, 'It ain't like that, man.' I'm telling you, whoever this chick is, she put it on him, gave that boy that act right, and he just been at the house chilling, checking his phone every fifty seconds," said Lynnesia.

"His first name is Jarvis?" Shakela inquired because she really only knew him as JAWS.

"Shut up, Kela. Look, I am going to be honest because it is just us in here, and I can trust y'all. Me and Jarvis been down almost two years. We haven't been intimate in a while but when we were it wasn't confusing because everybody knows. Jarvis is not a boyfriend he is the guy you call when your boyfriend won't act right. I mean it is college and everybody understands that. He doesn't do romance; he's the go to guy. He never wrote me anything, and he made sure I get out when we chill after sex! He used to make up somewhere to go when we first started, but then after some time of us having a thing, he admitted to me that he has a rule about girls spending the night. He avoids it at all cost so things do not get complicated," Tina rationalized, knowing the girls were all still trying to figure this out.

"You sure are quiet, Keisha, and you have something to say about ev-er-ree-thang!" Shakela said, rolling her neck as she clapped her hands to emphasize each syllable in *everything*. She looked upset with the world while borderline attacking Keisha.

"Tell the truth, Keish, what do you think? Do you think JAWS could be in love? I mean do you believe he is even capable of it?" Tina looked at Keisha sincerely as the girls awaited a response.

"Maybe he is in love, maybe he isn't; and you are right Shakela I don't have much to say about this. That is because I don't care. However, this movie is about to get good. It is getting close to my scene. I have to focus when Trey yells out 'Ricky' or I get all distraught thinking my baby died in real life. Y'all know he my favorite actor and he gonna ask me to marry him one day."

Keisha played it off without any hesitation or doubt from the other girls. Inside, she was secretly beaming. On the one hand, she really liked Jarvis; on the other hand, she had no idea it meant anything to him. She figured it was just one of those days for him. Because she thought he would not think much of it, she tried to take it the same way and did not let it eat away at her. She had dealt with it in her own way and really was over it before now. She just watched the movie with the girls and fell asleep peacefully.

A week went by. Keisha just returned to her normal routine. It was the week of homecoming at FAMU, so the city focused on the festivities. However, she was uninterested. She had her taste of college life on the wild side, and she wanted to get back to her goals. The thing that most interested her was accomplishing what she set out to do at the beginning of the semester and that was maintaining her place on the dean's list. That Friday, Keisha found herself in an odd situation. As she was leaving a study group in Tucker Hall, all of Tallahassee was on campus. People from all over had traveled to FAMU for the weekend— alumni, prospective students, and people who just wanted to be where the action was. There was no way for her to avoid the crowd. She had to walk through the set to get to her dorm room. *Well,* she thought, *I have done this a million times before; I've faced tougher challenges than this in life and succeeded.* She figured she would get tunnel vision and not stop until she was safely in her room away from the commotion. There was no way of doing that, though, after being spotted by friends from back home; she felt compelled to chat and be cordial. People who were yelling frantically because the Strikers and the drumline was performing on the set led by the drum majors right in front of the café. She noticed she happened to be in the middle of a crowd that was around one particular individual. It was Jarvis. People were going crazy over him. He had invited a popular musical guest, a rap group, and they had just finished shooting a major video that would bring all the right attention to FAMU and the band. This definitely cemented his status as legendary, and everyone just wanted to be around him. Keisha found herself caught in the madness. After about six minutes, it calmed down some. She happened to be by Jarvis and realized they had not spoken in about three weeks. She did not want to be rude, so she said to him in a cool tone, "Hi, Jarvis."

He replied, without really looking, "Hey, baby." He never even saw her. She was flabbergasted and just faded back into the crowd. Having no clue what to do, she tried to escape through the crowd but the scene bordered on insane, there was still no getting across The Set to her dorm room. No matter how she maneuvered, she ended up in too close a proximity to him and the mob that surrounded him. Jarvis stood tall, almost statuesque like an African warrior, just proudly breathing in the spectacle that he felt responsible for creating. He was unruffled by the crowd. His fellow drum majors surrounded him. One of them spotted an attractive girl in the crowd. She was in shape wearing a Florida State shirt. Morris yelled to Jarvis as he pointed in the crowd, "JAWS, it is blood in the water; freshman at your three o'clock. I know you been down because that girl ain't called you, but if that chick right there can't make you bounce back, nothing will."

Keisha felt stupid when she heard that. She really did not have the number anymore, and she wanted to reach out to him. Her feelings went from shame and humiliation, to anger and resentment. She was trying not to show any of it. She had no way to break out from the crowd without causing an even greater scene.

"Excuse me, baby, the head shark needs to see you!" one of the drum majors screamed to the girl in the Florida State shirt. Without delay, the crowd of men near Jarvis started in, almost like the most rehearsed choir, their moves like synchronized swimmers. "JAWS wants to take a bite out of you, and you better bite him back because once JAWS locks on you, you are going to get lockjaw. The man is named after the fiercest shark to ever live, and everybody knows sharks are born swimming. Come make a decision with your life, because it's a privilege just to go for a swim with the shark."

The lines were cheesy, and no one with self-respect would fall for that, Keisha thought. The young lady pointed to herself as if to say who me and look caught off guard. However, she got dressed that morning with this in mind and could not wait to meet JAWS. She held her friend's wrist and motioned toward the gathering of drum majors as if to say, "Let's go that way." She pivoted slowly to accentuate her assets. She was shaped like a Coke bottle, only curvier. She was fine. She walked toward the drum majors like the stallion she was, every step on point like a model hitting her mark. Keisha could not take any more of the scene, so she ducked out behind the drum majors and broke out. As she left, she heard Jarvis introducing himself to the young lady. "They call me JAWS, and I have just one question for you: Would you like to swim with the shark?" Keisha ran to her room and jumped in the bed. As she attempted to cry herself to sleep, she thought, *Oh, he's back to JAWS now. I thought he was only answering to Jarvis.*

That was almost three months ago. Now she sat in this doctor's office with the finality of the news from a medical professional. She had missed her cycle at least twice, from what she could remember. She also had proof from the two previous tests, but she was still hopeful that she would wake up from this nightmare unscathed. She felt forsaken and had no idea why this would be happening to her. Shook to her core, she felt things like this did not happen to people like her. Filled with more fear than ever before, Keisha walked out of the doctor's office with instructions in her hand and her heart in her shoe.

Dark Days Ahead

*K*eisha woke up the next day with a heavy heart, almost as if she was mourning her own death. An overpowering feeling of devastation was consuming her despite hours of meditation the night before. Nothing was working as far as making her feel OK. She would be fine for a few minutes, but would unravel with tears streaming down her face the next minute. In her adolescence, she envisioned pregnancy would be a happy time in her life after she was an established journalist and a fixture on network television. Never did she expect to be a statistic stuck in a gloomy dorm room, detached from the father of her child. She could no longer bear this alone and decided she would place one of the most difficult phone calls of her life. She called home.

"Hi, Keisha, baby. How are you doing this morning?"

"Hey, Momma"

"You know, I started to call you last night when I got home from Bible study, but I dozed off while watching them soaps I recorded."

"Oh, OK, Momma I called because I need to tell you something about what is—"

"Hold on, Keisha. Daddy just walked in, and he has wanted to talk to you," Mrs. Moore interrupted.

"Kee Kee, how you doing? I dropped by the bank and put a few dollars in your account. When you coming home?"

"School is out next week, G Poppa. I will be catching a ride back next Thursday with Lynn. You remember Mrs. Eula Mae's granddaughter?" Keisha told her grandfather.

"OK. Yeah, that is the pretty lil' girl that be with you; that is Elouise's daughter, ain't it?"

"Yes, sir, that is her. She is the one who does my hair."

"Well, hurry up and get here. I am going to let you finish talking to your momma. I love you more than you will ever know."

"Thank you for the money, G poppa. I love you more than the world." Keisha swallowed hard, feeling as if she was a disappointment. This was too difficult for her to continue.

"You wanted to tell me something, honey?" her mom said as she returned to the phone.

"Um, oh yeah. I just wanted to let you know that Lynn and I will be there next Thursday and that the semester is ending. I got to go, Momma. I have to run to the library to meet my study group."

"OK, baby. I love you, and I will see you on Thursday. I will cook a roast and scalloped potatoes, just the way you like them. So be ready when you get here," Mrs. Moore said. They ended their call in familiar fashion. Keisha wept inconsolably.

The next day, Keisha went in to work and wrapped up a few things. She gave her notice to leave the company when she met with Mr. Nathaniel James, the station manager. Mr. James signed off on all of Keisha's internship paperwork, told her what a marvelous job she had done throughout her time, and offered her a full-time position at the station. She had no choice but to turn it down, citing family obligations, and asked if she were able to return in the summertime, would the offer still stand. Mr. James let her know the offer was good as long as he was there because of her talent and work ethic.

News of Keisha leaving swiftly spread around the radio station. That day, she was eating lunch in the break room when Robert sat down beside her and began to pray over his food.

"Good afternoon, Robert. How are you feeling today?" Keisha asked as she sipped her tea.

"Honestly, I'm not doing too well. What about you?"

"I have been better, but I am starting to feel more positive about everything that is happening in my life. What is troubling you?"

"Well, you know this is not the biggest place on earth, and news is our business, so it travels fast. Mr. James informed me that you will be leaving soon, and I really do not like that. I had plans for you, and honestly, I was just waiting until you graduate. I thought me and you were going to take over the world, starting with this radio station. I'm feeling shattered inside."

"Don't worry too much, Robert. I am still graduating. I have finished all of my finals this week, and I put in the work, so I am confident I did well on those. I have completed my internship here. The only thing I have left is two courses, which I will finish next semester. I will be taking those online while I am back home, so I will be OK. I just need to be back home to take care of some family issues—nothing too major."

"Keisha, you know if you need anything, I'm here. Really, I am. You don't even have to ask. If there is something I can help you with, just tell me now, and I don't have to get all into your family business. Is it money or anything that you need? Is there anything would convince you to stay? I mean, if you need somewhere to live, I have a place here. Just let me know. Can I help in any way?" Robert was as sincere as he could be, almost desperate, as he eagerly anticipated Keisha's response, hoping there was some way he could come to her aid.

"Robert, you are truly a sweet guy, and I love you for that, but trust me, I am fine. Stand up and give me a hug. I just have some stuff I have to do back home. After the summer is over, I will assess my situation, and I may be back this way for graduate school. It is just family has to be my first priority," Keisha said as they hugged and concluded the conversation before returning to work.

Thursday morning came quicker than anticipated. Keisha gathered the last of her things in the dorm room and packed up the car. After taking in the dorm one last time, she realized the finality of it all.

During the ride, Keisha was preparing to tell her family the news that she had been concealing from them. She figured she would start with Lynnesia. It was time to face music, realizing she would be showing in a few months, if not in a few weeks.

"I have a confession, Lynn," Keisha calmly stated.

"Spill it, girl. This should help my driving and make the ride home go faster. What is it?" Lynnesia asked.

"I'm pregnant." Still trying to convince herself, Keisha was looking in the visor mirror as she repeated to Lynnesia, "I am pregnant, and I have not told my family yet."

Lynnesia looked at Keisha to see if she was being serious and then to check if she was OK. "Well Tina kind of hinted at something but I wasn't really sure; what are you going to do? Are you keeping it?"

"That option would never be considered an option for me, Lynn. You know better. It is way too late for that discussion anyway," Keisha replied in a matter-of-fact tone. They continued the discussion on the drive home.

Keisha moped around the house for a few days, wondering when was the perfect time to announce to her family that she was not returning to school, that she would be a mother soon, and even worse, that she was not engaged to, married, or on speaking terms with the father of the child. The last part would be the most disconcerting to her mother because Mrs. Moore was a widow. Keisha's biological father died when she was about seven years old. He was the reason she was so determined to make a future for the rest of her family. Her father was a veteran, a former Marine who had instilled a sense of loyalty in Keisha at a very young age. She always remembered that. She did not have many memories that stuck out to her more than her father's love for her mom. The way he would spontaneously dance with her mother in the kitchen or the living room. In the almost twelve years since his passing, Mrs. Moore never even considered dating as far as Keisha knew. She had to find a way to muster up the courage.

The Sunday before Christmas, Keisha sat down with her mom and G poppa and told them everything. They were beyond disappointed. G poppa had to restrain his daughter literally, who initially wanted to kill Keisha. Utensils flew from the table when Mrs. Moore stood and banged her fist down with fury unlike anything Keisha had ever seen.

"I know I won't be taking Pampers to the projects!" Mrs. Moore screamed as her father struggled to keep her away from Keisha.

"Calm down, Evelyn," G poppa instructed, as he grew tired.

"I did not raise you like this, Keisha!" Mrs. Moore cried out in anger.

"I'm so sorry, Momma. I didn't mean for this to happen like this. I promise I'm going to fix this. I'm still gonna graduate on time. I just don't know how to make this right. I need help." Keisha broke down and fell to her knees, weeping.

Her grandfather took control of the situation. They prayed and cried as the news worsened because of Keisha's lack of a relationship with the father. As time went on, the reality set in, and as a family, they were preparing for Keisha to be a mother. There was a family-first philosophy dominating their thought process. Eventually, the love overcame the stress of disappointment. They began accommodating the needs of what would be a new addition to the Moore household—that was to be celebrated. However, Keisha began to dive into a deep depression. She constantly wrote in her journals, something she had done since a small child. Sadly, the most recent entries in her journal were never positive. She absolutely dreaded being home. She finished her coursework early and was officially a graduate with a bachelor's in communications. She made a decision not to walk with her class because of her pregnancy. Being home, away from the atmosphere of college and having to see people from her past and explain why she was home working in the local drugstore, had taken a toll on Keisha's demeanor. She was depressed and feeling like a failure, which caused her to become unhealthy. Keisha was about three weeks from delivering her baby, and nothing made her better. She could not bear to tell anyone from school who the father of her child was; she made up a lie about her first love.

Meanwhile, Jarvis was gradually making a name for himself, hired by his uncle following graduation and producing several successful rap albums. He wrote a love song that received some national attention and critical acclaim. He was given the opportunity to manage a new artist at his uncle's label, Trisha Middleton, a sexy young woman that had a soulful voice. He put a pop twist on her music and she quickly became a star. He dropped a verse on her megahit single "Options" and that feature helped him become notable. They had a rumored romance that gave people something to gossip about while the song continued to rise up the charts. The song was everywhere, all over the radio and on TV.

After the success of that award winning song, Jarvis reached a different level. He established himself as a versatile writer and producer, a hit maker, someone that could compose a beautiful ballad or provide a hook for the most vicious rap record. Featured in several newspaper and magazine articles, Keisha clipped them and created something like a scrapbook of his accomplishments. She was disgusted with the idea of him, and the sight of him made her nauseous. However, any time she caught a glance of him either on TV or in an article, she was instantly fixated while being equally repulsed.

Her world came crashing down one particular morning when she wrote about her hate for him, which filled an entire journal. She had been vomiting all night, and she felt he was responsible for all of her pain. She began having negative thoughts about him being attacked by sharks as retribution for all of the evil things he had done to women. Keisha was in a very dark place, but there was no turning back.

Her last few doctor visits created some concern because of her lack of nourishment. Keisha was not eating properly despite her mother's delicious food. She was clearly malnourished to her doctor. She was in her final trimester, but had not gained a significant amount of weight, and her stress level was off the charts. Keisha was usually a joyous person, the kind who made other people cheerful just by being around her. She became the type of person who would clear a room with her presence just because one could feel the hate bouncing off her. She grew to despise Jarvis so much that she was holding on to hate and refusing to forgive him. It was literally making her sick. However, she was still gorgeous. Pregnancy added a natural glow to her, a radiance that made her more beautiful. It was like a little extra piece of Jesus shining from within that spread to her features. Keisha was naturally shapely, and men were drawn to her even in her pregnancy, which absolutely disgusted her. She never had a problem with her looks; she had always embraced the fullness of her shape. However, she had gained a few pounds, though not much, and felt fat. Therefore, the men that approached her during this time were doomed she immediately thought less of them. She thought they must be desperate for wanting to talk with the pregnant whale that she had become. She felt an incomparable despair. She stopped attending church, making up excuses about her feeling tired any time she felt pressured by her mom. Her lonely days grew to have more misery as she shut people out. She kept in touch with Robert the first few months she was home, but trailed off talking with him, as she grew weary of hearing about the radio station, notwithstanding his efforts to convince her to come back. Keisha became unrecognizable toward the end of her pregnancy—she was completely dull.

ALPHA AND OMEGA

The morning her water broke, Keisha was having trouble breathing. Her mother comforted her while holding her hand in the backseat as G poppa drove them to the hospital. Keisha looked at her mom and said, "I love you, Momma. I need you promise me something. Will you name my baby Madison Alexandria Moore?" Mrs. Moore nodded, thinking that her daughter was delirious. However, Keisha could feel something strange and knew she was near the end.

The baby was successfully delivered, but the wait afterward to see Keisha became unusually long. G poppa stopped a nurse and demanded that the doctor come inform them on the situation. The Moore's, a spiritual family of believers, did not lose faith. Mrs. Moore said a small prayer and sat quietly. The doctor came out of the double doors into the waiting area where they were seated. He looked at Mrs. Moore as he reached for her hand and then looked in G poppa's eyes as he began to speak. Mrs. Moore let out a blood-curdling "Noooooo!" The doctor looked at them while G poppa held on to his daughter as her shriek echoed throughout the hallway. "We tried everything, and there really was nothing more we could do. She fought hard, but she could not hold on any longer." Keisha died bringing Madison Alexandria Moore to life.

They welcomed Madison into the family and loved her even though every moment was a reminder of her mother. The joy Madison exuded was a delight. Still, Mrs. Moore struggled with the thought of having to raise a baby. The sight of Madison caused G poppa great pain. He was never the same after Keisha's funeral. He took ill a few years later and passed at the tender age of seventy-two. It was very difficult for Mrs. Moore to deal with the passing of two loved ones in about five years. However, raising Madison gave her the renewed strength she needed to push through her struggles.

Madison was a happy baby and seemed to grow up fast. Before they knew it, she was a young girl blazing her own trail. She was very athletic and equally brilliant as a middle-school child. She was always busy. If she was not playing in a basketball game, she was winning a science fair. Her ability to play instruments was prodigious, and matched only by her record-setting times at swim meets. Madison became an accomplished swimmer at a very young age and an expert at all strokes. She was a national champion in freestyle and butterfly. Madison entered high school with the all-American-girl-next-door tag and was every teacher's favorite. She was offered scholarships to several universities by her junior year of high school. However, she did not have to narrow anything down. Once the letter came from Tallahassee, she was locked in. A Rattler before she was born, it was in her blood and a part of the culture of the town where she was from. FAMU is the ultimate. Madison noticed that more of the successful professionals from her side of town were alumni of FAMU. The teachers, pharmacists, accountants, and engineers all seemed to have Rattler tags on the license plates of their luxury vehicles. They had a life that Madison could see herself living.

One morning, Madison came into the kitchen where Mrs. Moore was cooking. She asked something she had not done in maybe six years. Madison was sixteen now and grew more inquisitive about her parents.

Madison spoke to her grandmother in the most heartfelt tone although she did not want to disturb Mrs. Moore while cooking because that could end badly. Everyone knew not to bother her while she was in the kitchen creating a masterpiece, Mrs. Moore just might snap.

"Big Momma, what was my momma like?"

"Well, Maddie, baby, she was a lot like you are now!" Mrs. Moore wiped the sweat from her forehead, placed the spoon back in the bowl, stopped stirring, and then rested her hand on her hip as she sighed. "Phew. She did really well in school, never made less than an A on much of anything, and excelled in her extracurricular activities. She just wanted to be the best. She was filled with love and joy—just a pleasure to be around. Once she set a goal, she was driven to succeed. It did not take a push from me or anybody. She would set a goal, and then go get it. The best way to describe my baby was loving and driven."

"That's something I try to do, but I thought that was because you work so hard to make sure I have stuff. I just never want to let you down."

"Well, I appreciate that, Maddie. I really do, but a lot of that you got from your momma, baby. I have not been much help in the way of your studies. I ain't been able to help you with none of your homework since elementary school. The stuff they got y'all doing now is just different. You get in there and just knock it out. Your momma was the same way. Keisha would do all her work and then just write in them journals until she was blue in the face."

"What journals, Big Momma?"

"Them ones up in her room. They in that chest up there. Anything you want to know about Keisha you can find out in them writings, I'm sure. I ain't touched any of the stuff in that chest. I had the hardest time just getting rid of some of her clothes. I still do miss my Keisha Nicole—love that girl with all my heart. Without you and the good Lord who sees and knows all, I would have lost my mind a long time ago. The Lord knew that, too. That's why you here to help me keep my mind right, Maddie, and you do a good job of that."

"Can I go in there and read the journals from the chest, please?"

"Sure, baby. Just be careful with the stuff. I don't like to keep a messy house. I don't want to come in there and see stuff all over the place."

"Yes, ma'am," Madison said as she ran upstairs to the room where her mom's old things were. She was just being respectful. Mrs. Moore would never come in that room; she could not bear it. Madison was all she had left, and they loved each other in a special way. However, Madison knew she could get away with murder because her grandmother would cover for her.

Madison looked around the room and found the chest. It had a lock on it, but the key was on top, covered in dust. She blew off the key and opened it; inside she found more than thirty journals. She plopped down on the bed and began to read. From what she could understand, this volume had to be one of her mother's earlier writings. Some of the things that tipped her off were things that middle-school kids did in her mom's day were some of the things she and her friends did just a couple of years ago. She read for about two hours and got through three journals. When she finished, she was in a great mood. She reached for her cell phone and posted, "Feeling great today, the more things change the more they stay the same. #ILOVEUMOMMY #ripknm."

Madison continued to do well through her junior year of school. Throughout her senior year, when she had free time, she would often open up her mom's journals and just read. A healing and informative process by which she felt close to her mom; it helped her decide that she would live out many of the dreams her mom did not get to chase. Madison had many interests but decided to become a communications major, maybe do some sideline correspondence at the games, thus combining her love for sports and entertainment with her passion for writing and public speaking. She could possibly be the on-the-scene reporter for the local news when there was a breaking story, before hitting the anchor desk, and eventually the big time with her own talk show. She considered the endless possibilities, but Madison knew this was not just something she chose; rather, the career path had chosen her. She was in love with the thought of it because it made her feel so much closer to her mom.

Allow Me to Reintroduce Myself

"Right hand high look I must confess, swear to God it's time to get your momma a black dress. A 3-piece suit for your brother he gon' need a black vest. You have fucked with my family and my money now I gotta put three in your chest. Call the clean-up crew I'ma leave your whole block a damn mess; when I come through with the click clack there will be nothing left; nobody to retaliate, no bodies left. Everybody is getting bodied; a couple bodies at rest."

"Hold up Busy, I'm going to stop you right there, that was good but we need to come behind that on the back-up track and I want you to throw in some ad-libs starting after that second punchline. Your voice is already so powerful we need to soften up the track a little bit after that I can double up on that kick in the drums." Jarvis explained to Jay Busy, a national recording artist, as his phone rang. Typically, Jarvis kept his phone on vibrate and away from himself during studio sessions; he did not like interruptions while working. However, Morris

Bright was calling unexpectedly so Jarvis figured he should take the call to make sure this was not an emergency.

"Okay, I have to take this call though, everybody can take five and we will get right back to it once I finish this."

"Hello," Jarvis answered the phone.

"What's up brother?" Morris was happy to hear his friend's voice.

"Not too much brother I'm in Atlanta right now, in the studio putting the finishing touches on a project with Jay Busy."

"You working with Jay Busy, yo that is my dude man I love his music and he seems like a real one! You know like he really put that work in out there in the streets."

"Why because he's big and got tattoos? You better not believe everything you think you know, this dude went to private school and had a charmed life. This cat would not survive ten minutes in the hood for real. I can't begin to tell you how phony and fake half of this stuff is; this is exactly why I prefer working with singers. I know you didn't call me out of the blue to talk about these clowns, because some of these boys are real weirdos. What's on your mind, bruh?"

"I have an opportunity you may be interested in. There is an opening in the FAMU music department and I told them I know a guy! I think it would be perfect for you it is a music appreciation course; it would be your baby. You could basically create your own curriculum."

Jarvis briefly paused, and began reminiscing on his college days and thinking about his journey since then...

As time passed, Jarvis Alexander Williams became a superstar and developed a cult following. He left FAMU in fall 1998 and went on to do very well for himself in the music industry. He settled in Atlanta for the first few years out of school before buying homes in New York, Orlando, Miami, and Los Angeles. He traveled the world after a few years, making music and accomplishing many impressive feats. He was an award-winning producer and a highly requested songwriter, and commanded a hefty sum as a public speaker. He made his mark on the world, but he had always felt Tallahassee pulling on him; he wanted to come back "home to the hundred." He had donated a lot of money to the university over the years and been back to receive honors still it was not enough. He felt something was missing from his life. The thing that he needed more than being in the studio with great artists, on red carpets, and at award shows, was FAMU. There was something about being on campus at any school, and FAMU was home for Jarvis. It was where he became JAWS. That moniker was what his production company was founded under, it was how he promoted parties, and it was what made him. He wanted to return to Tallahassee, and the opportunity became available. It would add prestige to the university and provide that thing that Jarvis was looking for.

...he did not vacillate at all in his response. "Tell them to call me right away! I will take the position."

Once Jarvis concluded the call, he got back to his studio session that confirmed he was making the right decision. He really was becoming jaded with the music business. Jay Busy walked back in and began a conversation with Jarvis.

"Once we finish up here me and the fellas are going down to Buckhead for spa treatments, you are welcome to join us." Jay invited Jarvis out with his crew.

"Spa treatments, are you serious dude?" Jarvis surprised by what he was hearing inquired to see if Jay was pulling his leg.

"Yeah, don't knock it. Women love when men are well groomed and I need to be relaxed for the grind I have coming up, so I will be getting a manicure, a pedicure and a massage. I have a girl down there, who works wonders, you sure you don't want to join us? I have a racquetball game with my cousin Todd at 1:00 p.m. and we are meeting up after that."

"Man please, I am going to have to get a rain check on that one you can schedule me for Neveruary the 32nd for going with the boys to get a pedicure." Jarvis chuckled as he shook his head.

"Okay well let me know if you change your mind, Theresa, is a magician when it comes to getting out the kinks and removing tension. She is the queen of all masseuses." Jay finished asking Jarvis about the spa and went right back into music questions. "So as far as the ad-libs you want me just to add a few in for effect right?"

"That's right, I will add in sound effects for emphasis. What are your next few bars?"

Jay was back in the booth as Jarvis started back playing the track he was recording as Jay Busy went back into character and began with his deep voice and murderous lyrics.

"Kill a mother-fucker, you best believe I will; Jay gets busy in these streets 'cause Jay Busy trill. Pull up on you with 'my girlfriend' can't nothing stop her; I'm clearing out your block bussin' shots with this chopper."

Jarvis stopped recording, "Yeah see right there I will add in the sounds of the AK-47, so on the replay I am just going to let it play. You add in some grunts or just say yeah or we can really keep it real and I add in some racquet ball noises or some women in the salon talking about your crusty feet while they do your pedicure."

"Oh, I see you got jokes. Go ahead and do that, and we will see who will be laughing when the check don't clear. Stop playing and run the track I'm ready."

Jarvis finished that project and left Atlanta two weeks after that. When he arrived back in Tallahassee, he wanted his presence felt right away. After signing on with the school, finding a place to live, and redecorating his home, he felt settled enough. It was time to let people know he was formally back. He tweeted, "Meet me @Top Flight 2night, tag the owner. Everything is free bc it's all on me! Same thing next week @The Moon, Coliseum & Tabu. I'm back in Tally #JAWSRETURNS."

It was not a national trending topic, but it made enough waves to get people out of the house in Tallahassee that night. After arranging with the owners and promoters, Jarvis bought out the club that evening. He wanted to let everyone know he was back with authority. Arriving late to the club with an entourage, he did just that. The DJ announced him and let it be known that he was the reason there was no cover charge and all drinks were free. "Trap Queens and Hood Stars, put your bands away. Black bottle service all night courtesy of the legendary JAWS. Show him some love tonight. He is back in Tallahassee doing it like he used to." Jarvis laid back in VIP majority of the night before he worked the room.

Most of the night, he drank and shared stories with old friends from school and the band who were fully aware of his accomplishments. He was not ready to take down anything right away but just enjoying the night fully.

Jarvis attempted to school a few of the men he was with as they shared drinks while listening to the music. "Man, let me tell you, it ain't nothing like it was! Social media has changed the game. Got these very regular chickens thinking that they are superstars. They come in the club like they too good for anybody because these thirsty loners compliment them online."

"Facts, you telling the truth about that!" one of them agreed as he turned his bottle up.

"I know I ain't lying. I don't mind giving any woman attention, but some of them got the game all wrong, and the lames is the ones that's twisting they minds up."

"You right, you right." The men could not find a point to argue with because all of them shared the same frustration.

"Look here, man, I will tell them quick. I am too old to work for it. They know what this is. I be like, 'Girl, you are a receptionist. All you do is answer phones and talk to people all day.' If you're a cashier or a server, it is your job to talk to people, but now you walk in the club thinking you too good and instantly become the combination of some bad R&B chick, like you 'Chrisette Cole' or 'Rih-Yonce' or somebody. I know your body, right, but just because you got thirty thousand followers or two thousand likes on a picture, that don't mean I got to chase you. I mean, some of these girls are hustlers and parlay that thang into some real money. I don't hate on that, but use it for what it is supposed to be. Do not come into a social setting and be antisocial because you think you are a virtual star. You are not a model if you're only taking pictures on IG."

"Boy, I swear you preaching right now!" Marcus Johnson told him as he bopped his head to the music.

"Let me show you what I mean. You see that bad lil' red one right there?" Jarvis made Marcus aware of a nice-looking woman in the club. "She is thick and cute. I was chilling by the bar earlier. She came to me and spoke, and then she started singing some of my music. We had a nice little talk, and she gave me her number. She knows that she is going home with me tonight. The other one over there, though, is the one that I really wanted. The petite, brown-skinned chick—she is beautiful. I can tell, though, she going to make me work for it, and I ain't got the patience or the time."

"She is bad, though, I mean her skin and her features. She is just gorgeous. You sure she not worth the wait? The blacker the berry the sweeter the juice." Marcus quizzed.

"No doubt, she is bad but I am talking about what I want to happen tonight. Watch this. You'll see." Jarvis motioned for the first young lady whom he exchanged numbers with to come to him. Without hesitating, she came. "I just have one question for you."

She stopped him from talking by placing her index finger on his lips. "You don't even have to ask. I am ready to swim with the shark," she said proudly in a very erotic tone.

"Bruh, I am out of here. Y'all boys have fun parking-lot pimping." Jarvis clowned as he left, embracing and dapping down friends.

It was the perfect ending to the night. Tallahassee would know that he was back before classes were back in session. He met his goal and was ready to relive his glory days. He did not have to find the fountain of youth. He would be forever young at his home away from home. This was definitely what he was missing.

On campus, JAWS came back to life. He had been a fish out of water for a few years, but he was revered on campus. As a producer in the music business, he knew that when you get to his age, you are no longer the cool new sound anymore, and people are hesitant to call. He could always make a decent living writing and public speaking. However, coming back home was different; this was everything. New life was given to JAWS. Around campus, he was almost a deity; at functions in Tallahassee, he was no less than iconic. In conversations or sightings around town, he was legendary.

The rebirth of JAWS was similar to his first run. There is a groupie for everything, and the band has no shortage of them. The younger drum majors and professors who knew of the legend of JAWS and who absolutely idolized the man considered to have laid the foundation for them could not wait to pay homage to him by showing him the finest women they knew. Jarvis would frequently get calls from those looking to satisfy him. He had fun with it; his phone would ring almost daily with these types of calls.

"Hello, this is Professor Williams speaking. How may I help you?"

"Frat, what it is, baby? This is the eighth wonder of the world at your service."

"What's happening, lil' bro?"

"It is blood in the water!"

"Oh, really, so I take it you got something for me; well, I have just one question. Is she ready to go for a swim with the shark? Send her down to my office."

On the other hand, Jarvis Williams the professor was in a comfort zone like no other. His organic affinity for music made him one of the best professors anyone could have. He was an encyclopedia of music knowledge, and he could instantly recall any song, album, producer, or composer. In his class, students truly learned; however, the class was an elective. He was not that serious about the curriculum, even though one would think that he would be because he designed the course. He was friends with the dean and the president, so he was granted the leeway to do as he pleased. He enjoyed that kind of flexibility. His course had two major grades: the midterm paper and a final exam. The other assignments made up a measly 15 percent of the grade, whereas the midterm was worth 25 percent and the final covered the bulk of the grade. Despite his love of music and his vast knowledge of it, the course was the main breeding ground for JAWS. Not many men took his course, and if they did, they probably had a connection to the band or one of the athletic teams and just needed a grade. He had two teaching assistants—Kendra Jackson and Joy Lewis—both of whom he had ongoing intimate relationships with; they were his main scouts. Their jobs were to find and develop talent. They were there in the room to work for JAWS, not for Professor Williams. Jarvis thought the job was important; however, he used his position to fulfill his need to be JAWS. The course took place on Mondays, Wednesdays, and Fridays; Tuesdays and Thursdays, Professor Williams had office hours. The running joke on campus was the Friday music-appreciation course times. Everyone knew that there would be no class on Friday because Professor Williams started his weekend on Thursday night. Jarvis was truly happy again—he was at FAMU teaching the course with the freedom to maneuver as he pleased and not give up his life outside of the university. He maintained many of his connections in the industry, but FAMU rapidly returned as his first priority; everything else faded for him.

While immersing himself back into the culture of being a legendary Rattler, Jarvis took nothing for granted. He wanted to be everywhere that he could be to make sure he was fully enjoying the experience. If there was an event to be at, he was there. If there was no event taking place, he created one and properly promoted it until his function became the "it" thing to do. He turned up the vibe of the city and created a more profound name for himself with a new group of people. JAWS was still the man. He did not let a day go by where he did not promote his university or one of his businesses. Having the time of his life all over again, Professor Jarvis Williams got comfortable and felt untouchable.

On the rare occasion that he was not set up by one of his associates, he would approach women himself and expect them to almost bow to his self-perceived greatness. Jarvis was hanging in a lounge during happy hour, dressed in a suit but relaxed with a drink in his hand, standing a few feet from the bar when something caught his attention.

"Excuse me, my dear, do you mind if I have a word with you?" Jarvis leaned in toward a stunning young woman who had to be at least half his age.

"You would like to speak with me?" she responded almost with defiance.

"I just wanted to compliment you on your ensemble. You are well put together, and that combination of those heels with that dress is doing it for me. You look astonishing." Jarvis ran game like a sewing machine, just smooth and consistent.

The young lady chuckled and countered, "Why, thank you for noticing. You don't look half bad yourself. If you had on a tie, you would be overdressed, but that suit is wearing you. My name is Brandy, and you are?"

Jarvis gripped her extended hand and said as cockily as he could, "Allow me to introduce myself. I am Jarvis Williams. That's right, I am that Jarvis Williams, *the* one and only JAWS, and I just got one question: Are you ready to go for a swim with the shark?"

"I guess I may have some free time. Are you ready for me now?" Brandy replied.

He operated this way, almost living out a fantasy at this point in his life. However, this was his reality, and if an attractive woman happened to step in the water, then she was sure to be bitten by JAWS. He was back and loving every minute of it.

Madison Arrives

After graduating from high school, Madison left for FAMU in the summertime. She wanted to be acclimated as swiftly as possible and was never one to waste time. Her college experience was vastly different from her mother's. Always in control and never socially awkward, Madison was ready for the college atmosphere. She was a gregarious person, quick to make friends, and was the life of the party whenever she chose to be on the scene. Madison had an athletic body, but she was always feminine. She oozed sexiness and confidence. She was never promiscuous, but had experience because she was an extremely flirtatious girl. She always received attention, which she knew how to handle. Madison enjoyed summer school at FAMU, performing well in her classes, and began learning the city. Shopping was one of her favorite pastimes. After the passing of several of her family members, her grandmother set up a trust in her name from the insurance monies. Madison received a large sum on her eighteenth birthday with the rest to be released when she turned thirty-five. She was a fiscally responsible, almost frugal girl and was never impulsive with her purchases. However, she loved to be in style considered somewhat of a fashion expert by many of her friends. That combination of striking features, a shapely body, and a larger-than-life personality made her irresistible to men. Nonetheless, Madison never was preoccupied with any of it. Despite her being from a small town and constantly involved with structured activities, she was not a naïve freshman by any stretch of the imagination. She was born with game and could be considered somewhat of a heartbreaker—not cold but definitely ruthless. She would not embarrass a man as she manipulated him because that would be too obvious; she exercised discretion as a rule. Many men approached her, but she was never rude to the ones she turned down. She would curve them politely. They would walk away almost happy because they had the experience to speak with a lovely young lady and would repeat the excuse she gave them to themselves as if it made sense. Men would think to themselves, "She does kind of like me, but she has no time because of her studies," while nodding their heads in agreement as they muttered to themselves, "I really hope she does well." However, when she wanted a man's attention, she would get it without ever having to say anything. Madison could patiently make herself available to the man she desired at the time until he would take notice. Based on the conversation, she would then assess whether to rip the dude's heart out and show it to him or begin a romantic friendship. She ended her first year at FAMU with somewhat of a status of the girl who many of the popular men wanted. Her academics were the most important to her, so her social life was not a priority.

When her second year rolled around, Madison began to branch out. She had a core group of friends and even thought about joining a sorority. But much like her mother, she entered college with such a driven mind-set: the most important thing for her was finding a job in her field that would be a résumé builder for her career.

Madison did not believe that there was a man deserving of her undivided attention. She had not encountered a man who met all of her standards, so she created the perfect man by combining several of her male friends. That way, when one would fall short of her criteria, she could momentarily drop him and pick up another until he was necessary again. She had a texting buddy, one whom she would go to the movies with, a few to take her out to eat, and a friend who liked to take her on trips. She did not have an intimate relationship with any of those guys. Her friends who had benefits understood her lifestyle. She was involved with Tony, a football player from Florida State. They mutually agreed not to get too serious and that there was no need for a title on their relationship. Their arrangement was to remain casual, always protect themselves, and just call each other when there was a need without a lot pressure attached to their interaction. There was no drama if they would see each other in public with someone else or if they decided to get involved with or date someone else. She also had a friend from Miami, Fred, who would come into town occasionally on "business." He was a street-savvy fellow and was too charismatic for Madison to turn away. He was also the only man she had ever approached.

She went out to eat one day with a friend named Mike. Mike was a nice person; he had a secure teddy bear feel to him. He was a hefty fella that kept a well-trimmed fluffy beard. A man of few words but enjoyed a good meal; something Madison shared with him so their friendship developed around their love of fine dining. As they were studying the menu, Madison noticed a man not too far off in the distance attempting to flirt with her. She was accustomed to receiving this kind of attention, so it never struck her as odd. Although for some reason, this was different. The man that was looking at her was with a woman, and he did not seem to mind her knowing he was looking. When Mike saw him looking, he did not turn away to try to fake it. As her and Mike finished their food, they began to exit the restaurant; Mike, forever a gentleman, got up and pulled Madison's chair out in a chivalric fashion. Madison got up and took his hand as they walked toward the door.

Madison and Mike were about to leave the restaurant when an unfamiliar, almost strange voice stopped them in their tracks.

"Keisha? Keisha Nicole? My God, that has to be you!" The man who had been staring ran down toward Madison and Mike, blocking them from exiting.

"Excuse me, sir?" Madison looked dumbfounded at the man and sounded upset with him.

"Is there a problem here, fella?" Mike asked with a significant amount of bass in his voice, ready to defend the honor of the woman on his arm.

"No problem at all. Aw, man, it is just great to see you." He looked over Madison while shaking his head in disbelief. He was very emotional, almost pushed to the point of tears. "Forgive my manners, but you are Keisha Nicole Moore's baby girl. I see your momma all in your face. My name is Robert

Clark. Your momma was a good friend of mine, one of the best people I have ever met. You can call me Uncle Robert. Can I give you a hug? What is your name?" he said excitedly, rushing his words.

"My name is Madison. And yes, sir, I will give you a hug." They embraced for a moment. Madison felt a warmth and comfort with this man like nothing she had ever experienced.

"I apologize, Mike. Do you mind if I speak alone with Mr. Clark for a minute?"

"No problem at all. I will be right over here" Mike responded to Madison. The two men looked each other squarely in the eyes as they firmly shook hands before Mike granted them some privacy.

"I don't want to take up too much of your time. I just could not take my eyes off you all night."

Madison had heard that line almost a thousand times but never like this. The sincerity that Robert spoke with touched her. He held her shoulders tightly while looking her over as if to check she was real. Nothing about this encounter was sexual. He was awestruck. Typically, Madison would have been nonchalant and aloof, but this time, she was flushed with emotion.

"Honestly, Mr. Clark, I detected you observing me, and I thought it was kind of weird at first. Now I see why you were looking," she explained.

"What are you doing here? Are you in school? You know if you need anything—and I mean anything—I can take care of it. I'm connected up here. Your uncle Robert is only a call away."

"Well, Mr. Clark, I am at FAMU. This is my second full year actually on campus, but I am finishing the last few credit hours of my communications degree. I came into school with credits from dual enrollment, and I have been looking for a job."

"My God, you are your momma's child. Say no more, though. A job in communications—you're hired." He handed her a card from his coat pocket. "Call me tomorrow morning, no matter what you're doing, and e-mail your résumé tonight."

As Madison read the card, she noticed the title of the company, Clark Media Solutions. Her newfound "Uncle Robert" was the owner and CEO of his company. Madison instantly understood the significance of this. She hugged him again and said, "Thanks, Uncle Robert."

"Baby, come take this picture for me." He motioned to the woman over at the table to come over to where they were. As he introduced her to Madison, his face beamed with joy. "You are looking at my newest radio personality and television reporter. I am going to fast track her like nobody's business. We are going to be able to compete with 102.3, and she is going to make the network pop!"

Madison whipped out her phone and took a few pictures with Robert. She added it to her story and updating all of her statuses. "New Beginnings #omw" was how she captioned the picture. Her comment section was active because all of Tallahassee seemed to know her uncle Robert. He now owned a radio station after spending years working for one. In addition to the radio station, he developed a site with impressive online content about music, fashion, and entertainment. He was also in the early stages of developing a television network. He had a local news show and a few start-up sitcoms that were doing OK as far as ratings.

Madison had been working with Clark Media Solutions almost a month, being trained by the best and developing her own style. She had a knack for the industry and felt accomplished, as if she was making her mother proud. That fulfillment gave her an indescribable peace. She learned the entire behind-the-scenes work first and began working her way to the other side. Robert quickly showed her the ropes; he had plans for her to become the face of his company.

A year later, Madison became the voice of the radio rush-hour show, carving out a comfortable niche and somewhat of a name for herself. She was also progressing with television, which seemed to be her true passion. Initially, she thought she was chasing her mother's dream, but she felt alive in front of the camera. It had hidden intrinsic rewards, and she truly enjoyed all she was doing. Her academic course load lightened; she was balancing all of her responsibilities well and never had an issue doing it. Toward the end of her third year in school, she met with her academic advisor, who informed her that she had satisfied all of the necessary requirements to graduate. The only thing she was missing was an official on-the-record internship, and she could log those hours while working at her job. After she completed that, one elective would do the trick in her final semester.

Once she had developed a routine at school and work, it became a piece of cake, and she had a lot of downtime. During those times, she would snuggle up with one of Keisha's journals and just learn something new about her mom. She was finally able to convince her grandmother to let her have the chest full of her mother's things. She kept the chest in the bedroom of her apartment, away from people. It was in those private, intimate moments that she felt tranquility. That was, until she began to make disturbing discoveries. Madison learned about her mother's college years and an experience she had had with a guy who had shamed her mother. The story was filled with anger, and the humiliation her mom felt leaped off the page and into her heart. As she was reading she thought to herself, *I cannot believe this creep did not have the decency to acknowledge my momma after they had relations. What a scumbag!* Madison stopped with that story on that day and felt anger toward all men for some reason. However, she continued with her normal routine, but began to detect a hint of bitterness toward men throughout her daily interactions. The natural distrust she had for them became more obvious; she had heard more than enough stories from friends and knew to watch out for them even though she was in charge of her emotions and had never been played by a guy.

One day, she realized she was changing on a customary trip to the grocery store. She had an uncharacteristic exchange with an older man who was attempting to be pleasant with her. She was in the express checkout line behind this gentleman, and they were both purchasing some of the same items, which was why he struck up conversation with her.

"This pollen is the worst this time of year, huh?" the man commented.

"Are you talking to me?" Madison almost snapped at the man.

"Yes, I am. I saw that you have some of the same allergy medicines I have. I have such difficulty breathing during this time of year. I come outside, and my car has a yellowish-green tint to it, and I have sneeze attacks for no reason."

Although Madison completely related to and usually made people feel at home even under the most stressful situations, she rudely responded, "Do you have twelve items? The sign clearly says ten or fewer, and I am kind of in a rush. You sure do talk a lot for somebody who can't breathe well."

The man looked confused and just said, "I am sorry to bother you."

Madison thought about the incident on her stuffy drive home because she had difficulty breathing through the heavy pollenated air. The epiphany that the story in the journal was starting to take effect on her made her want to read more of the journals to see if she could change her mood. She unloaded her groceries, put on soft music from her favorite Pandora channel, and fixed herself a drink before she rummaged through the bottom of the chest. She read about twenty-four of the thirty-something journals and neatly organized the ones she had finished. They were sacred writings; she never shared what she had read with anyone. Only she and her grandmother knew about the journals. When she began reading the latest journal, she became optimistic that the entries she discovered were about her mom being pregnant with her. First off, she read about the devastation of having to tell G poppa and Momma Moore. Then she was excited to see that her mother had a resilient spirit and that she had created a plan and was going to use her birth as the motivating factor to get back on track. After a few pages about refocused plans, the writing became depressing. It was obvious to Madison that her mother had begun to starve herself during certain periods. Being back in her hometown was tantamount to life imprisonment for her mother. Her mother saw no way out financially and thought that her dreams of being a national talk-show host and media mogul were over; she did not see herself even making it to a major city and being a reporter. Madison felt guilty and angry, almost as if she had ruined her mother's life. As she read on, she saw several moments where her mom spoke of her love for her unborn child and that the little girl was the only hope she was holding on to; that lessened Madison's guilt but not all of her anger. She drank herself to sleep that night and woke up the next morning with the same feeling of disgust. Trying to find a way to calm her nerves, she went for a drive. When she was out, she called up a friend.

"Tiffany, girl, what are you doing?"

"Not too much, just out running errands. What's up?"

"I am over off Park Avenue heading to Governor's Square. I need to clear my mind, and I was seeing if you were available to meet up."

"I am over off Tharpe Street, not too far from Old Bainbridge. I was just over on Apalachee Parkway paying my cell phone bill, but I can turn around. I will meet you there in a few."

"OK. I'll be in the food court and will grab some bourbon chicken while I wait on you."

The girls shopped, and that was therapeutic for Madison. She was sponsoring Tiffany for the day, so it was definitely not an issue to accompany her on the retail therapy trip. They talked, and Madison's mind was free from the anger for a moment. As they left the mall, Madison began to see the words from the pages of the journal scroll across her mind. She just listened to music softly as she headed back home, attempting to find some serenity.

Madison continued with her life, but her anger never truly subsided. She read a few more of the journals over the course of the next month, which proved to be a very unhealthy practice. It did not affect her performance at work, but it began to take a toll on her personal life. She had all but cut her relationship with Tony. He was an undrafted free agent who finally made an NFL roster but took more of an interest in Madison. He attempted to develop more of their relationship, seeing if it could progress from their original arrangement. He made many attempts to reach out to Madison, but one day, her frustration reached a maximum. She simply sent him a text that read, "It is best that we do not waste any more of each other's time."

Fred was the one who was always able to keep Madison's interest, but she was annoyed with him, too. She stopped responding to his texts and phone calls without cause. Fred never pressured Madison and just let her be herself. He never understood the reason for the breakup; however, he did not stress it. He knew Madison was young, and he would eventually have her interest again. He decided to give her the space he thought was necessary and stopped reaching out after a while.

The distance from the guys she had been involved with created a problem for Madison. She did not have many positive substantive relationships outside of her work dealings with men, which were not meaningful relationships. Many men still made advances or did their best to get to know her, but Madison had already shifted her focus. She just wanted to finish her degree and begin pursuing her career goals

CLASS IS IN SESSION

*M*adison entered her last semester of college ready for graduation and ready to move on in life. She had her job under control and began an upbeat path. She resumed her social-life, hitting the club scene on occasion before classes re-started and attending a few functions, including the freshman showcase, which was electric and put her in a great mood. It was about to be football season, and the city would be alive. As her advisor counseled, she took only one course that did not require a lot of work—Music Appreciation, taught by Jarvis Alexander Williams.

When she entered the class on the first day, she sat at the end of a row near the back, wanting to go unnoticed. As the rel-atively large class with roughly 150 students packed in and took their seats, women outnumbered the men with nearly a two to one ratio. In grandiose fashion, the door opened. The students were silent as Professor Williams began shouting across the Perry Paige auditorium, which was an odd place for this class, but it was one of Jarvis's requests. He began to stalk the crowd like a comedian in control of his audience. The way he paced back and forth demanded a certain level of respect and undivided attention. "My name is Professor Jarvis Williams, and I am your instructor for Music Appreciation. In this course, you will learn the history of music. You will learn how it is the heartbeat of the world at large. The impact great musicians have made over time, and you will understand what all genres of music have in common. Music is the voice of God speaking to your soul; it is how we most freely express our love, and it is my life. I have had the pleasure of studying some of the historically great musicians and the geniuses of our time from FAMU's very own Dr. William P. Foster to Johann Sebastian Bach, from the incomparable Michael Jackson to the great Quincy Jones, the unique impact of Kirk Franklin to the unrivaled creativity of Robert Kelly. We will dive into all music, and we will have fun. My teaching assistants, Ms. Kendra Jackson and Ms. Joy Lewis, will be the main facilitators of this course; those are the two ladies passing out the course syllabi for any of you who could not download it or print it. I plan to waste none of your time, and I will not allow you to waste any of mine. This course will be stimulating and challenging. There is a midterm and a final. To meet the requirements to pass this course, you must be present on those days and those days only. The other days that the course meets are for lecture and debate to help you understand the concepts that will be tested. My office hours are from six o'clock to eight o'clock in the evenings on Tuesdays and Thursdays. You can schedule appointments with Ms. Lewis or Ms. Jackson. Your first assignment is due today. You are to answer the questions that I put before you now: What would the world be without music, and what does it mean to you specifically? Turn your papers in to the assistants as you exit. I look forward to serving you this semester."

Madison placed the final additions on her paper and handed it to Ms. Jackson, who was in a discussion with one of the students that Madison could overhear. "He is certainly going to meet with you next Tuesday. Can you come by at six? It will be the last time you have to see this course, and you will have a definite A for the entire course! Just answer this one question: 'Are you ready to swim with the shark?'" Madison was sickened and hurriedly left the room.

Wednesday rolled around, and the class had dwindled to fewer than seventy people. It was obvious that the given assignments required little to no reading and that this course was a facade—a way to keep Jarvis Williams occupied while they paid him. Madison was frustrated with this sham, and she could not believe her university would participate in this kind of nonsense. The academic integrity was one issue; the other issue was the overall immorality of this geezer preying on young women with the help of these two dopes he called assistants. The entire farce upset Madison, and she did not need any more fuel.

After class that day, Madison continued her usual routine but that night she decided to read a few of her mother's writings. She snuggled up with one of the few remaining journals and this particular entry was something that tipped her off and drove her to her limits of fury. She began to see a similar trend from previous entries during her mother's final college days and her time of pregnancy. There was a deep depression apparent in the tone of the entries; the more she read, the more she realized that the guy from the earlier story who had humiliated her mother was liable for this madness and that he was most likely her father. Madison dug deeper into her investigation and began to see a very familiar face. The iconic Jarvis Alexander Williams had to be the man from Madison Street with whom her mom was so upset. She found newspaper clippings and magazine articles. She grew more incensed the more she discovered. She could not believe what she was reading but as she pieced it together, her view of her current professor drastically changed. Once perceived as a man whom she respected as an alumnus who made something of his life now became hatred for the dead-beat father he never was to her and the jerk he was to her mother. Her disgust for Jarvis Williams became similar to her mother's obsession, and that was the only perspective she had on the scope of men at the time. She began to have a new goal in life. Based on her mother's writings, she wanted to see Jarvis Williams in pain. Her rage that night was almost palpable but she had no healthy way to vent. No one she trusted enough to talk to and no positive interactions with males to balance these feelings at the time. Her mind began to go into a weird thought process, after about an hour she felt drained emotionally and physically weak, and without much of a choice she went to bed.

About five weeks into the course, Jarvis began to take an interest in Madison. He noticed her coming and going and how pretty she was; he wondered why she had not been by his office. Ms. Lewis was observant and catered to Jarvis' needs; in her mind, that was her man, and she would do whatever was necessary to satisfy him. Before he could request, Ms. Lewis approached Madison and began to talk to her.

"Hi, my name is Joy. I do not believe we have actually met. I have graded a lot of your essays, and your stuff is really good. But you know you really should not be working this hard."

"Is that so? Why do you say that?" Madison asked as she folded her arms.

"Well, if you are able to stop by the office this Thursday, your A will be guaranteed. I mean, with all of the work you have done up to this point, if you are able to complete a question-and-answer session in the office, you would be exempt from the final."

"That is generous of you, Joy, but I work on Thursdays. I'll just keep putting in the work if it is all the same to you, but I do appreciate you informing me," Madison curved Joy and left her feeling anything but rejected. As Madison left, she could see Jarvis and Joy speaking about her. She did not pay much attention to the conversation and went about her day.

Madison realized what happened to her that day in class after she was approached and did not recover from it well. One night when she was already at a tipping point, she decided to finish reading the journals only having two left to read. She was hopeful that near the end of the pregnancy that she would read something in her mom's demeanor that would give her some reason to talk with her father or to be positive in general. She was intentionally looking for something encouraging that would provide her some peace and she could move on from this or possibly reconcile it all. The journal that she picked up seemed to be buried at the bottom of the chest. Madison previously did her best to organize them chronologically but this one must have slipped by her. However, what she read sent her over the edge.

Wednesday - January 20, 1999

Dear Diary,

I finally mustered up the courage to reach out to Jarvis and I am on my way to Tallahassee to finish our conversation. I told him that I needed to talk to him and he actually remembered me. The conversation went well, much better than I anticipated. I was too nervous to drop it all on him at once. I am really hoping the trip goes well and we have some type of relationship where we are able to converse peacefully and at least co-parent. I have been in deep meditation about this and I am still scared out of my mind, I don't know what to expect when I get there. I have so many thoughts and fluctuating emotions flowing through me. At times, I'm excited, then anxious, fearful turns to cheerful but mostly I get worried because of the unexpected. This is all in addition to being hormonal because of the pregnancy. Thank goodness, I haven't began to show yet. I am going to remain cautiously optimistic I'm keeping an open mind. I'm just going to see how this goes. I am staying with Tina at her apartment it will be great to see her and few more of my friends. She will be going out of town with her boyfriend. I will have the place to myself for a few days.

Thursday, January 21, 1999

Dear Diary,

Had a great time with Tina yesterday, it has just done me good to be back in this atmosphere. It seems silly the stuff that you don't even realize you miss. I knew I missed some of the food places but just being on the campus, walking in Tucker hall, and riding the shuttle was cool for me. I'm going to meet with Jarvis again. He came by right as Tina was leaving with her boyfriend. Jarvis and Tina spoke for a brief moment. Then he and I watched TV together. We had a great talk early in the day and he came back that night and spent the night with me after he came from the club. We shared a few passionate kisses but he seems to have grown and matured somewhat. We actually talked about dating like being a real couple. He is living in Atlanta now and said he thought it would be great if I came to live with him. I don't know if I'm expecting too much too fast but we really have a great vibe. It is just like it was when I first met him; the time seems to be at a standstill and nothing else in the world matters. I know he really likes me, it is so obvious in our conversations. I think he and I could actually have a future. I mean he has graduated. He is already becoming successful, I love his ambition and I know we can be great parents. I haven't told him about my baby yet, wait, our baby, but I am debating if I should let him know tonight, when he gets back. I am almost certain I am. I don't want to drop this bomb on him in a strange way but he deserves the right to know. I have told Tina she was shocked to hear that Jarvis would be the dad but I believe talking with her has eased some of my fears. Met with Robert for lunch he really has been such a good friend to me and I was able to hang out on campus for a little while. I will be going to the radio station tomorrow and checking into some options for graduate school. It was a great day I am very happy that I made this trip.

Friday, January 22, 1999

Dear Diary,

    Crying my eyes out as I sit here at the Greyhound station. I walked here from Tina's apartment. The day started out great; got a lot accomplished as far as checking into graduate school but I didn't realize that Tina would make it back from her trip early with her boyfriend, apparently her and Jarvis were not over each other. I can't believe I confided in her and she still would do this to me. I walked in on her and Jarvis going at it and the worst part is once they saw me they only paused. He had to nerve to insinuate that I should join them. I left that key and I didn't turn back; he drove his truck to come after me but I didn't want to talk. I have never been more devastated in my life. I have no idea how I got myself into this mess. I thought he was a changed man and she used to be one of my closest friends. He has hurt me again and I didn't think it was possible for me to open up to even be hurt, but I don't know how I can go on from here. I just want to disappear. I don't want to talk to anybody or do anything.

The journal entry continued and it was clear. This moment drove her mother into darkness. Madison now had concrete proof that Jarvis was her father and drove her mother sick. She was enraged initially but then became composed and calculated. She continued coming to class just to learn the tendencies of Jarvis Williams. She watched the way he moved, how he interacted when he was flirtatious. Overall, she hated to acknowledge that when given a real question by one of the male music majors in the course who actually wanted to learn about music, He was well-versed in all facets and gave outstanding advice and pointers with insight into the business side of the industry. Madison had to admit it; Jarvis was intellectually captivating. He easily held the attention of everyone in the room and commanded a certain level of respect. She did not want to, but she liked that about him. That infuriated Madison even further because she saw the potential of not only the class but of the man. He had allowed his promiscuous nature to dominate what he could have been; despite his many accomplishments, he was not half the man he should have been in her eyes. With all the pain he had caused to the many women he had taken advantage of, she considered him downright pathetic.

The weeks passed. On the Monday of the Florida Classic week, Professor Williams announced that classes would be canceled that Wednesday and Friday and would resume the week after Thanksgiving with the final taking place on the seventh of next month. The course for all purposes was pretty much over. Madison needed an acceptable grade on the final in order to pass the course, graduate with honors, and continue on the path that her mother had intended. Typically, when she ended a course, she would greet a professor and thank him or her for his or her time if she had not introduced herself earlier. The majority of her classes were small enough that she met some of her professors prior to the class ending because her work stood out, and usually she was actively participating in class. This time would be different. She walked out unceremoniously in a bittersweet moment. It should have been filled with elation. She walked out of that room with a quiet confidence knowing that her very long, difficult journey had ended and that very soon she would be accepting a diploma making Big Momma very proud and living out her mother's dream. She also felt the moment was soured because her father, a man she barely knew, was teaching the class that was at the conclusion of her arduous road. It should have been celebratory and satisfying, something she could share with him, but it was really just another pleasurable opportunity that he had ruined. Her college days concluded with this slime-ball making life miserable, yet again.

They Meet

*M*adison, asked by Mr. Clark to do a piece on the classic, decided to close her show with what she created:

Epic is one of the most inappropriately overused words in the English language. People use it to overrate their experiences, food, and routine events. Nevertheless, if you were to describe the Florida Classic, an annual football game played between the Wildcats of Bethune Cookman University and the Rattlers of Florida Agricultural & Mechanical University, you would have to start with the word epic, *which does not really cover it. You could be as redundant and dramatic as you like and call it the Super Epic, Gigantic, Colossal, Larger-Than-Life, Blockbuster, Extravaganza Classic. That still would not do it. Almost nothing compares to being a student in the prime of your life at the university you idolized as a child and being at the classic. You have to wait your entire life to get there, and to be there and live in the moment is just, well, epic. It is truly deferred gratification.*

There is no real way to describe what the classic is like for someone who has never been; not accurately, words are inadequate.
It is like the explosion of the collision of the homecomings of both
schools. There are the step shows, The Battle of the Bands, the car
shows, the parties, major artists doing concerts at nightclubs,
and so much more. The football game is probably the least emphasized of all the festivities that surround the week. The rivalry
began as far back as 1925 and became an official classic when
they chose a stable site in 1978 in Tampa, and then moved it
to Orlando in 1997, where the game has been held ever since.
On average, there are about seventy thousand people in atten-
dance. However, outside the stadium there are probably twice as
many people tailgating. Lake Lorna Doone is where you can
find most people; packed with people having a good time. The
sounds of Frankie Beverly & Maze, along with Earth, Wind &
Fire, followed by the Isley Brothers blare through speakers to give
the moment a soundtrack. Even when it is raining, you still see
our people hanging out with new hairstyles. Blocks and blocks
of vendors surround the stadium. The tradition of the classic
combined with the atmosphere of the people, some of whom have
never attended nor visited either of the schools but support them
with the same amount of loyalty and spirit. The city, filled with
cars flying school flags and an ocean of orange-and-green with
maroon-and-gold waves. High school and middle school bands
from around the state come to participate in the parades and
battles. Tampa Avenue is covered with people patronizing the
vendors looking for the perfect T-shirt to commemorate the event
or the right funnel cake. Lines pack to capacity as people wait
for their barbecue or fish sandwich to finish cooking, and in the
neighboring tent, paraphernalia of the Divine Nine is sold. The

unofficial hood car show takes place with the nicest rides playing the latest music and displaying their brand-new rims. It is like the ultimate family reunion mixed with great music, laughter, and events that make lifelong memories. The camaraderie is inexplicable to those who have not experienced it. The on-the-field rivalry is fierce, but is surpassed by the love of the common struggle, and it all culminates with one thing—the halftime show. The display of talent and culture that all come together with a twenty-minute performance from each school's respective marching band. I cannot wait to see you there, Rattlers.

Madison was preparing to travel to Orlando with friends for the classic. They were on all the right VIP lists for the clubs they wanted to attend. When she arrived on Friday night, she had more fun than she could imagine with her friends and was in the best of moods. Saturday rolled around; it was game day. She and her girls walked down Church Street after parking and headed to the Citrus Bowl. They stopped to take selfies and group photos, and they flooded timelines with nonstop pictures. "The definition of fleek," captioned by Morgan, was a group picture of all four of the girls that hit the one thousand like mark before they entered the game. Madison was feeling great, and the game helped her mood. Tiffany, always camera ready, never stopped snapping photos. She took about sixty pictures with Morgan, Madison, and Jada as she pretended to watch the game, trying to find the perfect shot to make it look like she had a natural one-take beauty.

"This is the one, girl. Look how great we look in this. Do you like it?" she asked Madison.

"It's cool. You can use that one," Madison replied.

Tiffany began typing in her phone, trying to find the perfect thing to say. "The Fleekingtons!" We aren't just family…we are famuly #TURNT #Classiclife #Collegegirls. #Rattlerbeauties @ Morgan_freewoman @MaddiefromTally @Jay2much."

"This is the one that will break the Internet," Tiffany said to the girls, sounding pleased with herself.

Jada and Tiffany were looking down her timeline when they came to a picture of Jay Busy. "Oh, double tap on that one! You see bae staring at me with his shirt off."

Tiffany scoffed at Jada, and turned to the other girls saying, "Do you see this? Jada is trying to claim my man, Girl bye, you know better. You know that's bae, I know that's bae and more importantly he know he bae. You saw when he responded to my post because he is always my MCM."

"All he said was 'thanks' you acting like you are in some deep talks with him." Jada put Tiffany in her place. "You talking about that's bae; the only b.a.e. you know is bacon and eggs. You can't afford for that booty to get no bigger, you are one meal away from being big. I was trying to be nice but you came for my man. You are going to make me get ugly."

"I don't have to make you get ugly. God already did that take several seats." They playfully roasted each other still having a good time.

"All of this over some dude that neither one of you know nor is he thinking about either one of you." Morgan put a stop to the joking because it was starting to become vicious.

At halftime, Bethune Cookman went on first, and the crowd went absolutely nuts following their performance. However, the anticipation of FAMU's performance was palpable the energy was ridiculous. As the Marching 100 got into their positions around the football field, it was as if time froze. The pandemonium that engulfed the stadium seemed to be different from the other years. The irreplaceable Joe Bullard began to introduce the halftime lineup as the drum major whistles filled the air and the drumline struck up the band.

"From the highest of the seven hills of Tallahassee, transmitting Rattler pride…Often imitated but never duplicated." Joe Bullard's voice is as distinctly powerful as it is distinguished. FAMU is the greatest band to take a field, and they did not need the extra help. Nevertheless, he is the perfect complement to the band. The Marching 100 shut down the Citrus Bowl. Usually, there was some debate over who won the halftime show because it was far more important than the actual score of the game. However, as the band rattled, marched, and danced, the debate ended before it started. Even Cookman fans could not hide their adoration. After halftime, the girls were ready to participate in the customary stroll around the stadium to see and be seen.

Down on the field, Jarvis watched the halftime show with a conceit that poked his chest out to a new level. His arrogance was fueled by that performance. The band pleased him that day. The band was a part of the reason he came back and he assisted them in his free time.

He walked down from the luxury press box that he typically would spend the whole game in before the start of the second quarter and was ready to head back up to his seat. However, he was in such a good mood that he figured he would walk around, see what the atmosphere was like, and hear people talk about the band with hysteria and fondness. He bumped into an old friend while heading toward a concession stand under the bleachers.

"Leon Johnson, *we back, baby!* That is the FAM I always want to see from here on out."

"I know, that's right!" his old friend Leon said with a smile as the two men dapped each other while embracing. "They look good out there. I said to myself, 'Now JAWS been whipping them into shape like Doc had us.'"

"You better know it. We're back, and I mean we are here to stay," Jarvis told Leon.

"I know, I know. I saw them hitting those nineties when they needed to, and I heard that sound quality and it looked like it was 'bout fifty tubas. It is good to see you, brother. I am going to get back to the Mrs. Johnson with these nachos before she start barking and blowing up my phone."

Jarvis continued around the stadium. Overflowing with happiness and now in a nacho kind of mood once he heard his friend mention it, he came to a concession stand and decided to pick up a bite to eat. He left the concession stand, chomped down on his food, and guzzled a drink until a former student who knew him on a personal level stopped him.

"JAWS, I know you down here getting it in."

"Well, I may have put in a little work last night. You know how it is."

"I know how it is for you; was she bad?"

"Oh yeah, she is bad now but when I tell you it got *ugly*, boy, I mean it got *ugg-uh-lay*. Met her at the party and took her back to my place I got here on the east side. She was sipping on Patrón before we got there, so she was ready. I went in the bathroom and came out with church socks and a wristwatch on. I just let her look for a minute, and then I asked her while I was pointing to my watch. I said, 'You know what time it is, don't you?' Then

I answered for her. I told her 'it's time to take a swim with the shark.' I let her have it."

"You are a straight fool." The young man laughed wildly as he listened to the story that sounded like a fairy tale, but he knew every word of it was true.

He spoke with the young man for a while longer until he noticed someone out of the corner of his eye. He hastily wrapped up the conversation and walked in the direction that had his attention.

"Excuse me; you are in my class, aren't you?"

"Well, at the moment I'm not. I am just waiting for my friends to come out of the bathroom. I was in your class until you basically announced that there was no more class for this semester."

"Well, not really. We will meet a few more times just to review for the final, but it will not be too tough. My name is Professor Williams. You can call me Jarvis."

"OK, Professor Williams. We can just keep it at that. My name is Madison. It is nice to meet you. I'll see you around."

"The pleasure belongs to me. Maybe when we get back to Tallahassee we can hang out, you know, after the final."

"That should not be a problem."

"Here is my number, call me anytime."

"OK. I will text you mine."

Jarvis walked off with a strut that let him know it was certified at this point as he received the text from Madison. Now he has her number, and she has his. He had been eyeing Madison for weeks; she was his number one target.

Madison went back up to her seat where the girls had been patiently waiting for her.

"You been gone for quite a while, Madison. You just left us after we all used the bathroom. I was starting to get worried about you," Jada said. "Is everything OK?"

"Yeah, everything is cool. I saw an opportunity that I needed to take advantage of, so I made myself available for it. It would not have worked if we were in a group. That's the only reason I split off like that, but I am here now," Madison responded honestly to alleviate any concerns for her well-being.

"You are the slickest person I ever met. I don't even want to know what you are up to," Morgan said.

"That's good because I'm not about to tell you." Madison smirked.

"You are so sneaky." Morgan just shook her head.

"Not sneaky, discrete. You will not see anything about me on Yeti." Madison replied.

The girls watched a little more of the game before they left the stadium. The rest of the weekend went according to plan. They partied at the clubs and had fun drinking, dancing, and meeting people. The party lasted into the morning when they sat at a diner laughing and reminiscing on the weekend as if it all took place years ago. After the late-night/early morning breakfast, they returned to the hotel where they rested before checking out and driving back to Tallahassee.

The Chase

After Madison returned to Tallahassee that Sunday, she be-gan to pack to go home and visit her grandmother for Thanksgiving. Knowing she would be back in Tallahassee in only a few days, Madison prepared for a light week of work. Her phone rang. It was Jada.

"Hey, girl, what are you doing?" Jada asked.

"I just finished loading up some stuff to go home on Wednesday. Now I am working out—nothing major."

"That's what I need to be doing, but I can't hang with you. You go so hard. What are you doing? Maybe I could join you?"

"I was in the middle of getting dressed, but I was going to run two miles, get in about five hundred abs afterward, and then come back and finish my workout DVD."

"What do you mean five hundred abs, are you talking about sit-ups?"

"No, I hate sit-ups!"

"Me too girl, I just rather do jumping jacks or something. All that struggling to get off the ground, but I could not do five hundred of them bad boys."

"No, silly, I meant I hate sit-ups because they are not as effective as the other exercises I will be doing. When I say abs, I just mean any abdomen exercise. Like today, I will more than likely do some V-ups, bicycles, crunches, twists, and hangmen. I need to get my core back tight. You know everything starts with your core."

"Again, I can't hang with you. You are always running five Ks and all that other stuff. I am not about that life. I don't even know what half of the stuff you just said means. I will go down to the fitness center here at my complex and walk on the treadmill. You inspired me to do at least that. Are you competing in a triathlon or another one of those events you like?"

"I have something big I am preparing for. I am glad that you are going to get on the treadmill. Every little bit counts. That is a great thing for you to do. Bye, girly."

Madison hung up the phone, smashed her workout, came back to the house, and settled in for the night. As she sat there, eating on the couch and catching up on favorite shows on her DVR, her phone went off. It was a text from Jarvis.

Hey, I was just thinking of you.

She deliberately waited about ninety minutes before she responded. *Oh, that is nice. Thank you.*

About twenty minutes elapsed before she received a response. *Are you busy? This is Jarvis, you know. Not sure if you locked me in your phone.*

I know who you are, Professor Williams, and I am somewhat busy. I have a really big final coming up for this course I am enrolled in, and I hear it is going to be tough. LOL☺

ROTFL! The final is a piece of cake. You have nothing to worry about, since that is the case, would you like to go for a drink and hang out for a while?

Madison made him wait again. After about ten minutes, she responded. *Maybe some other time, I have settled in for the night, and I cannot see me getting up and going out for the night.*

Oh yeah, that is cool. It was probably a long weekend for you. Get you some rest and just let me know when you are available. Jarvis gave Madison an excuse for her not wanting to meet up—as if she needed one.

I can do that. I will probably give you a call after I return from Thanksgiving and see what you are up to then.

OK, that will work. Jarvis did not want to appear needy, so he tried to let it die at that. Still, he figured he would try for a Hail Mary. *I am out driving. I could always just stop by.*

No need, Madison quickly replied. She was definitely not giving out her address.

Well, good night, get you some rest and sleep well. I know I will have pleasant dreams about a young lady I met during halftime at the classic. Jarvis wanted to see if Madison would throw him some kind of hint that she was interested.

K was all she gave him about fifteen minutes after his final text.

Jarvis sat at home staring at his phone, reviewing the thread of messages to see what he should have said differently or if he could infer something cute from what she said to him. "I probably should not have lied about being out. She may be thinking I am up to something. I probably should text her back and say I am home now. But it is too late, and I told her good night already. I don't want to look like a stalker," he mumbled to himself for nearly half the night before he fell asleep.

The next morning, Madison was up early eating breakfast and preparing for her run. She returned from exercising earlier than anticipated and felt well. Realizing she still had more time before she needed to get to work, Madison decided to go down to the pool in her apartment complex and get a few laps in. That turned into forty-five minutes of swimming and a water workout. She got back in her apartment and showered before heading off to work. When she got there, she began her normal duties. At about 11:45 a.m., her phone buzzed.

Good morning, beautiful, how are you is what the text message read.

She responded back immediately. *I'm fine and you?*

I am good, just relaxing at my place, been working on a song that I am writing for a friend of mine in the industry.

Oh, that's cool. Well, I'm at work. I will get back with you in a little while when I take my lunch break.

That will work.

Jarvis eagerly waited by his phone, anticipating a text message around noon or maybe in the one-o'clock hour, but nothing came. He decided to go about his day like normal even though he could not really think straight because of Madison. He wanted to know what he could do to get her attention, because nothing seemed to be working. Putting in work for some chick was just not something he normally did. He sat at home after going through his day, watching *Monday Night Football* when his phone rang. He looked at the screen. It was Madison. He was shocked but tried to play it cool.

"Hello, this is Professor Williams. How can I help you?" He adopted a Barry White bass to his voice in an attempt to appear laid-back.

"Hi, this is Madison."

"Oh, hey, how are you?"

"I am doing well. I called because I wanted to apologize. I got really busy, and before I knew it, I never took a lunch. I keep my word, though. I did not want you to think I forgot you."

"That is no problem. I barely thought about it. I know what it is like to be busy. What are you doing now?"

"I am still working, and I am glad you understand. I will talk with you tomorrow. I have a deadline to meet. Bye," Madison said before hanging up.

Jarvis just sat there, looking at his phone in amazement. "Did that just happen?" he asked himself. He could not believe the call he had waited all day for was over before it ever started. Jarvis became a little unsure of himself, not certain of what he was doing wrong with this girl. However, he knew that he had to have her. Over the next few days, Madison and Jarvis exchanged pleasantries through text messages with Madison keeping him successfully at bay. Thursday rolled around, and Madison headed home. She arrived at her grandmother's house around 1:30 p.m. to the aroma of a Thanksgiving feast.

"Big Momma?"

"Maddie, baby, is that you?"

"Yes, ma'am, it is!"

Madison and Mrs. Moore hugged each other tightly for a very long time. Madison washed up and set the table as instructed. Mrs. Moore had really outdone herself. Everyone raved about her cooking, and she earned that. All of her meals were delicious; no one had to embellish to make her feel good. Clean plates were her most frequent compliment. The doorbell rang throughout the day as family and friends stopped by to enjoy the Thanksgiving meal. While watching the football game and placing the food back in the refrigerator, Mrs. Moore began singing; she was in a great mood now that her granddaughter was back in town.

"How long you staying this time, Maddie?"

"Well, I will be here a few days. I got a few things to take care of when I get back, but they could be delayed without any trouble if you want me to be here with you a few extra days."

"That sure would delight my heart, baby! It does me good to see you and have you around."

"Well, I need to leave Saturday morning, but I can stay through Tuesday if you can do me a tiny favor."

"What you need from me, chyle? I will do it if it will keep you here."

"Well let me explain." Madison and Mrs. Moore sat down ate slices of pie and talked for about an hour.

"Thanks, Big Momma. It will be about two weeks from now. I don't want you to forget on me."

"Chyle, please, I don't forget a thing. You ain't never seen nobody in their sixties look this good, and I am still sharp as a tack. I ain't just fine. I'm smart, too. That's where y'all get it from. You are not the only one who can set up a plan. I will remember."

Madison burst into laughter and again replied, "Thanks, Big Momma."

They cleaned and spent time together watching television in the living room. Mrs. Moore caught Madison up on the latest news at church, while Madison lay on the couch with her phone in her hand, half listening to her grandmother, scrolling down her time line liking random pictures. Mrs. Moore was in hog heaven spending time with her granddaughter. She lasted as long as she could, but soon drifted off to sleep in her favorite chair. Madison woke her up and walked her to bed. Madison got in a brief workout and went to sleep herself.

Early the next morning, Madison was up, but not for the sales like most avid shoppers. She went for a run and a swim. Her regimen in the morning became more strenuous as she began incorporating weights into her training. Later in the day, Madison went out to pick up a few things but did not stop by the mall. The crowds and the frenzy over cheap electronics did not excite her. She stopped by a sporting goods store and picked up some jump ropes, a backpack, new shoes (a pair of aqua socks), disposable shoe covers, a razor blade, a water-resistant stopwatch, and gloves. She really seemed to be upping her workouts.

On the way home, she stopped by a local car rental place and rented a vehicle. There were no other customers, and only one customer service agent was available. She had a friendly conversation with the woman helping her.

"Welcome to Speedy Car Rentals. My name is Jazmine. How may I help you?"

"I need something roomy like a sedan, and I am going to need it for an extended period of time."

"How long is an extended period time?"

"Maybe like a month. Can I return it sooner if I need to?"

"Sure. Just fill out these forms. If you have it that long, you have to pay extra for the insurance. I hope that is not an issue."

"Actually, it is not an issue at all. I have the cash now to cover it." Money was never an issue for Madison; it had no value to her. She was usually tight with it, but spent it freely when she considered it necessary. "Can I pick it up tomorrow even though I am paying now? What are your business hours?"

"That is not a problem at all. We are open from eleven in the morning to eleven in the evening daily. Actually, you can pick up or drop off at any time as long as your paperwork is complete and the car is returned without damage and with the proper amount of gas. We leave the lot open because sometimes people return cars during hours we are not open, and we have that drop box for the keys right by the door. Let me take you outside so you can look at our vast selection of cars." Jazmine joked with Madison because of the limited amount of sedans in Speedy Car Rentals' collection. "We are not really a huge lot. I mean, we are like a lot of businesses around here. We don't even have surveillance cameras, like the little gas station down the street."

"I noticed that," Madison said.

"You can have the red one or the blue one."

"I will take the keys to that one over there. Is there anything else I have to do?"

"Just give me a minute to grab the keys and look over the car with you, and you can be on your way."

After the inspection and receiving the sedan keys from Jazmine, Madison took the short drive back home to spend more time with her grandmother. She was showered with love and food from Mrs. Moore while back at home. Madison drove her grandmother around later that day as Mrs. Moore bragged to all her friends how her grandbaby was in town spoiling her.

Madison loved seeing her grandmother happy. It was pleasing to be in the company of family. Neither of them spent much time with anyone else, so this was a mutually special bond. Madison knew that her grandmother's love for her was unconditional, and she needed that; it was the driving force in her life combined with, the wind beneath her wings, the will to see her mother's dreams come true.

When they returned home from running errands, Madison changed into her workout clothes. At this point, she was in full training regimen. She swam wearing her new aqua socks with dumbbells in her hands, which were to provide her with a little extra weight. After the cardio, she got into some of her ab routine and then ran back home and did some light weight training to a workout DVD. She showered afterward and just relaxed in her grandmother's room, talking her to sleep. She continued to enjoy the weekend, maximizing her time with workouts and making sure her grandmother was taken care of and did everything she wanted, which meant going to church and Sunday dinner.

Monday morning, she made a phone call as she sat on the couch finishing her breakfast.

"Good morning. Lynn's Hair and Nails, Ana speaking. How may I help you?"

"Yes, may I speak to Mrs. Lynnesia please?"

"One moment please. May I ask who is calling?"

"It is Madison Moore."

After a brief pause, Lynnesia came to the phone. "Maddie, I was wondering who would be asking for Mrs. Lynnesia. Since when have you stopped calling me Ti Ti Lynn? You better not be in town and not come to see me."

"I been here with Big Momma, Auntie Lynn. I need a hair appointment if you have one available. Do you think you can fit me in sometime in the next two days?"

"Oh really, so now you need an appointment to come see me? I ought to hurt you, lil' girl. You better act like you got some sense, as smart as you are. Whenever you come out here, I will put you in my chair, and you know that. You just as slick as you want to be, but you can't fool me. I know you are always up to something. You were always plotting and scheming all the time, don't forget I used to change your nasty lil' diapers."

"Don't do me like that, Auntie. You know your salon is way out in west nowhere. I can't just drop by like it's down the street. If I can get out there, will you bring me back to Big Momma's house?"

"My salon is strategically placed out here by the pier on the edge of town so I can catch the beachgoers and the people from the neighboring cities that know how good my work is. Anyway, I can do that. I have not seen Momma Moore in a good minute. I need to be ashamed of myself while I am around here talking about you. What did she cook? Please, tell me she made a pumpkin pie."

"There are still some leftovers from Thanksgiving and some other food. I will wrap you up some stuff now, and I will be to your shop in a few hours after my workout, around three o'clock."

Madison finished her breakfast and changed into some running clothes. She let her grandmother know that she was off to get her hair done after she completed training. She took the keys to the rental car and her book bag. She stuffed the book bag with towels, clothes, a large gym bag, and miscellaneous items so that she could weigh it down while she was running. Madison always looked for ways to increase the burn in her workout. She jogged about a mile and a half to the car rental place and rested. She entered the car and drove down to the pier while blasting the AC to cool down. Once she got to the pier, Madison unloaded the items from the bag into the trunk of the car. Afterward, she got into the water, took a swim, came back, rested, and did it all over again. She was timing herself and was content with her times, so she decided to leave the ocean and finish her workout with a run to the salon. As they rode back to her grandmother's house, Madison was feeling content, she had her hair done and enjoyed her time with her aunt. Lynnesia sat and talked with them while she ate pie and then left with the things Madison wrapped up for her.

"You tell Elouise I said hey and be safe, baby," Mrs. Moore said to Lynn as she got into her car.

"Yes, ma'am. I love you both. I know you loving how I laid your hair, Maddie!" Lynnesia waved as she drove away.

Madison got up early the next morning. She ran up to her mom's former room and picked through the drawers containing G poppa's old things. She was careful not to wake her grandmother until she had fully packed her car. After she was fully loaded, she reminded her grandmother of the instructions and drove back to Tallahassee.

THE SETUP

"What's up, man? What you doing?" Jarvis asked Morris as soon as he answered the phone.

"Leaving campus, I was parked over by the stadium, so I am about to turn on to Wahnish Way. Why, what's going on with you?"

"I am over by Monroe now. I had some business to handle out by Capitol Circle, but I wanted to link up and talk to you, man. My mind all over the place, and I don't know what's up with me right now. I just don't feel like myself. It may be because I am hungry."

"I am free right now. We can meet if you want."

"OK. Meet me right there on Macomb and Tennessee. Pick me up a two-piece spicy meal with fries, dark meat, with a sweet tea and whatever you want. I got it when I get there."

"Now, you know I don't eat like that anymore, and I got you."

Morris walked into the fast-food restaurant and ordered the food while waiting for Jarvis. He was slightly thrown off by the employees at the counter. Their disposition struck him as a little too comfortable to be at work.

The woman behind the counter was polite, beaming an eye-catching smile, but was still unprofessional. "Hey, I'm Meka." She smacked the roof of her mouth with her tongue making a familiar annoying clicking sound as she spoke. (mturk) "How can I help you today? Would you like to try one of our combo meals?"

"I would like a two-piece spicy meal, dark meat, with fries and a sweet tea as a drink, please," Morris said as he attempted to compose himself.

"Um, we ain't got no dark meat in spicy right now. It will be about fifteen minutes 'cause Craig just dropped some."

"OK, that's fine. I will have the white meat."

"We ain't got all the white meat right now either. (mturk) I can get you a spicy wing and a mild leg if you want."

Flabbergasted at this point, Morris could not hide his disgust. *Did she just say that they have no chicken ready, and that is what they serve?* Morris uttered in his head. The wrinkles in his forehead were emphasized as he raised both of his eyebrows in amazement. "I will just wait the fifteen minutes."

(mturk) "OK, thank you, sir. If you have a seat, (mturk) I will bring it to you when the food is ready," Meka instructed Morris as she began rapidly tapping herself in the top of her head.

As Morris sat down to wait for the food, Jarvis pulled up and parked. He entered and sat down across the table from him.

"What's going on, fool?" Jarvis asked as he gave Morris their ritualistic handshake.

"Not too much but waiting on your chicken. By the way, they have no chicken ready at a chicken place. Here is your cup."

As amused as Jarvis was with the circumstances and his friend's frustrations, he didn't comment on that. Instead, Jarvis explained why he had called Morris and what had been troubling him.

"I do not know what's up with me!"

"What do you mean?" Morris inquired.

"I mean, do not get me wrong here. I am thankful to God for all he has blessed me with, and trust me, I know I truly am blessed. But I just feel like something is missing. I mean, when you called me to come back to Tallahassee a few years ago, I thought that I had completely filled the void in my life. It has been great being back here. At first I had a few doubts, but they went away. After assisting the band, being able to be back spreading my knowledge and love for music, I thought I would be complete. Plus, you know the added perks of being JAWS in my old stomping ground. I thought this would be it, but something is missing."

"What do you think it is?"

"Do you remember how excited I was when you got me back here when you first called?" Jarvis asked. "It is that feeling that is what I'm missing. I have just been bugged out. Nothing really excites me anymore. I think I really want to settle down. I want a family. I am ready to change, mold a young mind to conquer the world."

"Whaaaaat? It is about time!"

As the two men dove deeper in the conversation, they noticed a considerable amount of time had elapsed. About twenty minutes into it, Meka placed a tray of food on the table.

"What did you tell her I wanted?" Jarvis asked after he had looked over the food.

"A two-piece spicy dark meat, that is white meat, and it does not look spicy; plus they got you mashed potatoes instead of fries."

"Excuse me, darling, can you come back for a second?" Jarvis called out to Meka.

(mturk) "You talking to me" Meka asked as she began to slap the top of her scalp mercilessly. "Oooh, my head itching! (mturk) Anyways, what you want?"

"Would you do me a favor, darling? Will you refill this for me with a lot of ice and take this?" Jarvis handed her his cup and a hundred-dollar bill as tip.

Meka returned with the drink. She was still slapping her head in an almost-cruel fashion. "I told Craig he got your order wrong, but anyways, um yeah, thank you for the tip and stuff."

Jarvis thanked Meka for returning the drink and chomped away at his food unbothered by the inaccuracy of the order. "It's OK, baby. Don't worry about it. You keep that and give Craig this." He handed her another hundred. Meka went back behind the counter, almost skipping because she was so happy.

"You realize you just reinforced bad customer service for the next person who comes off the street who does not have two hundred dollars to tip," Morris said in an aggravated tone.

"I cannot worry about that. I have real problems. I met a girl, and I think I am ready to settle down and stop doing what I usually do."

"Stop doing what you do or stop being who you are? No man can change unless he truly wants to. So before you give me some story about a girl that I truly have no interest in hearing about; why are you ready to change?"

"Honestly? Because it is time, I look at what you have. You have a family. I look at all the greats at FAMU, and there are a lot of them. I wanted to be notable, leave a legacy, put my name beside the greats—Dr. William P. Foster, Andre Dawson, Marquise Grissom, Dr. Fred Humphries, Willie Galimore, Bob Hayes, Common…"

"Man, you see what William Packer and Rob Hardy are doing. Nate Newton, Althea Gibson, and John W. Thompson are legendary. Keith Clinkscales and Rico Love are making their marks. People absolutely love K. Michelle," Morris said as he backed up Jarvis's point.

"There are too many people to name, once you start you will unintentionally forget someone, but I can tell you understand what I'm saying. I wanted my name mentioned in that sentence, and I thought that would be enough for me. Now I want kids. I want to live forever that way, not just be immortal through my works. I want to build a family legacy."

"OK. You may be ready, but do me a favor: don't tell me anything about this woman until y'all have actually dated for more than a month. Because you weren't always like this, you have not been this way since your first love. Back when we were crabs you were a loyal boyfriend, but you changed. I think I remember bits and pieces of what happened with you and Christie but never really the whole story. What actually happened? Why did you change?"

"I changed because life changed me. You are right when we were freshmen I was that man. Remember we used to hang out with Charles, Torey, Geno, and the rest of them boys from Paddyfote. There was one time after we went to a party in Palmetto South; it was some girls having a crab boil or something. You know it was a big deal because we got a ride on the back of a pickup truck; remember it was that rule that freshman weren't allowed to have cars. But when we got to the party, it was a few bad chicks there; one of them really liked me but I explained to her that my girl was back home and I was faithful to her. We came back from that party and I called my girl Christie she and I would have astronomical phone bills and that was with the ten cents a minute from 1-800-collect and phone cards. But that day she was acting strange, so when I came to visit her that weekend, she revealed to me that she was feeling the distance and she wasn't sure if she could trust me. The next morning was her birthday so I was going to surprise her with a breakfast to start the day. I go over there early that morning and I see my homeboy Garrett's car in the driveway. Her grandmother wasn't in town so I went to the door and these fools left it unlocked. I turned the doorknob and I see him smashing her up against the wall. At first, I lost it. I was ready to spaz on her and him but I felt an odd calmness come over me like a burden had been lifted. He looked like a deer caught in the headlights. He and I went back to the 9th grade. If we were going to play a girl that would be one thing but he had been dropping salt for months, lying on me to get close to her. She literally jumped off this fool and just cried with her hands in her face. I looked. Thought about killing them and just walked out. He tried to talk to me on the way out and she blew my phone up for the next three weeks before I actually answered her. At first, I laughed about it on the ride to my house because it was only four minutes away. But on the way back to school I was trapped alone with my thoughts and memories of our relationship and I cried for maybe an hour on my way back to Tallahassee. Because it finally hit me that I truly loved her and she loved me, but I knew if she had it in her that none of the women I dealt with could be trusted. From that moment, I vowed never to be a boyfriend again. So I just told women upfront what time it was with me and that opened me up to all the women I had been ignoring. After she admitted to me all that she had been doing, she wanted to work it out. I never looked at her the same again, and for that matter not any other woman."

"Yeah that definitely changed you. You became a beast in your sophomore year. The only thing I cared about during my sophomore year was making sure none of my classes interfered with my TV schedule. I had to see Jerry in the day to see two girls fight over some dude that was their roommate and catch Free on 106 and Park."

"Not just that it was a few things that shaped the way I looked at the world and women."

"Don't you really mean the shape of women is all you look at in the world? You became a monster after that no little bad chick is safe. All she has to be is light skin, young, and near you. After that it is a wrap!"

"I don't discriminate in anyway. I don't know if you remember A Tribe Called Quest but I'm just like that. 'I like 'em Brown, Yellow, Puerto Rican or Haitian; name is Phife Dawg from the Zulu Nation.' Or like Wu Tang 'French Vanilla, Butter Pecan, Chocolate Deluxe even Caramel sundaes is getting touched.' All flavors, colors can get it; did I ever tell you about the night of the hurricane when the girls from Florida State came looking for Peyton?"

"Peyton, you mean the white boy that sold weed in the apartment above us. Man, he was my boy; just super cool we would watch football together all the time, all day on Saturdays and on Monday nights. No you never told me about that, what about it?"

"Well at the time I was kicking it with Simone mainly and she was calling me nonstop that day but I didn't want to get stuck with her all weekend. I heard a knock at the door and it was three aerobics instructors looking for Peyton. I let them know they had the wrong apartment and I walked them upstairs to show them where his apartment was. He wasn't home and they asked me if I wanted to come out with them. I went with them to the liquor store as the rain started; the wind wasn't that bad to start. When we got back to their dorm room, the weather was crazy it started as a severe thunderstorm but the point is we were stuck in the room all night with a case of beer and some other drinks. They started getting frisky with each other and me. I took turns pleasing all three. I thrashed them I felt like I had to represent for all brothers but when the weather calmed down I left their dorm and began walking home. On my way home, Simone popped up out of nowhere she asked where I had been. I rode home with her and she needed some attention so I touched her up too, all in the same night."

"Boy you have lived a crazy life, most men dream about the stupid stuff you have actually done."

"Man it got crazy for me after me and Trisha ended our little fling; she fell in love with me when I produced her album. It didn't last long though because she fell in love with the next guy that wrote her a hit. That was kind of her thing she is still a free spirit. After the success of that record, girls would just walk up to me reciting lyrics getting most of them wrong. Asking me stuff like can we go island hopping, I will smile all day while we shop. I honestly stop remembering names and most of the faces start to look the same. The lifestyle just got too wild at one point when I would tour with artist. The things girls would do to get on the bus or up to a hotel room were ridiculous, then they would see me later in the mall or something and say things like 'do you remember me from Chicago; I was the one who came to your room with just a bathrobe.' I would seriously have to think to myself, the one that came to my room on Friday or Saturday because I really did not have a clue. I would just nod and play it off make and small talk, then back out of the conversation smoothly."

"It's like every time you talk and tell one of these stories I just wish you were lying but I know they are true."

"Well then, you know that I don't discriminate; anybody can be a victim, I take no prisoners. A woman can even be ugly but at that point, they need some special talent. Either know how to change a tire or fix a ham sandwich with the perfect amount of mustard and mayonnaise. She don't have to be young either, what really shaped me was my English professor. After Christie and I tried to make it work because she begged and begged, I was just open to whatever came my way. I took notice of how my English professor would give me special attention. She would act as if my answers were on track even if I was way off or as if my questions were so profound. One day after she released us, I helped her with her things when I walked her to her car. First, she told me she noticed how popular I was and let me know that she attended one of the recent games mentioning that she was impressed by my performance. Then she asked me how I made ends meet while in college. I told her how Doc and a few others let me do odd jobs and landscaping work for them. Finally, she mentioned some yardwork that needed tending to at her place. When I got there, I put some mulch in her front yard. About ten minutes after that her ex-husband pulled up and took the kids for the weekend, and she called me in once I was finished and paid me. We were deep in conversation when she asked if I would like to shower up and I told her that I would. I called for her when I got back to the shower and told her that I needed help getting the water hot; of course, I was naked, and to my surprise, she was too. We got in the shower and she taught me lessons; more hands on and different lessons from the ones that she taught in class. She put me up on so much game. She taught me more about how to treat a woman and not to always be a machine. She was fifteen years older than I was and had so much life experience. She was accomplished in many areas."

"When did you stop messing with her?"

"Truth be told I beat her four months ago; that's what I'm telling you. I don't have to have a young girl. You know she is up in age now. That night she thought she was going to have trouble physically so when she called I honestly just went over to check on her. She had some health problems in the past, an irregular heartbeat and some other stuff, so we were driving to the hospital to get her checked out in the ER. On the way there she started to get hot and began rubbing on me, I seriously thought she was trying just to reach for my leg to help her not be as nervous. I wasn't paying much attention because I was driving and I wanted to comfort her. I was trying to watch the road, you know. We in the parking lot and she already had me riled up. I asked her if she was feeling better and she told me she was but wanted to stay a while to make sure. I pulled her panties to the side and we didn't even get in the back seat. She sat up on me and I beat the brakes off her. The whole time I was tripping though, because I kept hearing this weird jingling noise. You know I usually keep my keys in my pocket and play with them from time to time but they were not in there so I just kept looking around. I could not find anything but I kept hearing the noise. I finally broke down and asked her what it was. She was just bouncing but then she stopped and the noise stopped. I said 'did you hear it?' and she was like 'oh that is just the rods in my hips.' I was like man this is crazy but I kept beating it until she couldn't take anymore. Her heart ended up beating too fast so she had to go in the ER anyway. I left her there."

"I am going to get out of here. I got to get home now," Morris said as he and Jarvis embraced while still laughing.

Jarvis finished his food and left. He got a text message from Madison asking if they could converse tomorrow after class. He agreed and went home cheerful. The next day, he sat patiently in a room full of students. Jarvis concluded class and was approached by Madison. He walked her to her car as they talked and set up an actual date for that Friday. Friday came, and they met for lunch. Madison allowed Jarvis to talk about his experience in the music business, his time out on tour, and his speaking engagements. She was very brief with her responses, but Jarvis continued to grow fond of her. He was really starting to gain an appreciation for her and the things he did get to know. It made him want her more, but he was not in attack mode. He never could discern why something was different about their relationship. However, he still felt a very strong attraction to her. After eating lunch, they hugged and set up another date for that Monday after the final exam.

Again, Jarvis waited in the class, but was more anxious this time. He and Madison exchanged smiles as she entered the room. He made the final a simple essay question about what the students learned and how they planned to share their new-found appreciation citing examples from the lecture materials and presentations from the course. Typically, when students have what are considered cupcake courses that sound like they are not challenging, the professor can be authoritarian and guarantee that students have a difficult time, almost to gain a reputation as if he or she has to legitimize his or her course by ensuring the work was ten times more difficult than was necessary. Jarvis was always reasonable because he had nothing to prove. He just wanted the essay to be over and the class to be done so that he could spend more time with Madison, because he knew she had to go in to work that day. After all of the essays were completed, Madison and Jarvis went for a walk around campus. They bumped into Jonathan Bertrand and his team, they filled out some surveys and had a discussion with him about the effects of social media before they continued strolling the grounds. Jarvis asked Madison if she would be willing to go to the beach with him on Thursday. She waffled and told him that she was not sure if this was a good week for her, because she would be taking her car home the next morning and traveling back to Tallahassee on Wednesday afternoon, so she would probably be tired. He tried to impress upon her how much fun they could have out in the ocean, and that it was magnificent deep out in the sea. She told him that she would let him know.

Over the next two days, Madison and Jarvis messaged each other, with Madison becoming more flirtatious. Jarvis began to realize that all of the other women he dealt with had fallen off. He had not been active for weeks now, and he was really starting to dig Madison. At the end of their discussion on Wednesday afternoon, Madison informed Jarvis that she was actually free for the weekend starting on Thursday. Jarvis reminded Madison of the beach offer. She messaged him again, declining the offer to the beach, saying she was just too tired. However, Madison called Jarvis back shortly after that final message and said she might have some energy and that she was thinking the beach could be fun and relaxing out on his boat. He asked her to come along again. She was sluggish and undecided in her response, but after some time and multiple requests, she accepted. She gave Jarvis her address late Wednesday night and informed him that she would be ready any time after 3:30 p.m. Jarvis was ecstatic and began planning things in his mind. That Thursday would be a huge day for him.

I Have Just One Question for You

That Thursday morning, Jarvis got up early and made sure his boat was securely attached to his truck in preparation for his trip with Madison. He told his assistant to give him a call around ten that night, because he would be occupied for most of the day. He picked up Madison around 4:00 p.m. They drove for about an hour and a half to the dock where Jarvis planned for them to leave. Madison had fallen asleep, tightly clinching her bag and snoring somewhat. When they pulled in to park, Madison slowly began to awaken. Jarvis carefully backed his truck into a parking space between a red sedan and a grey SUV. The FAMU tag on the front of his truck shone brightly, almost as if it was smiling.

Madison yawned and stretched. As she got out of the truck, she readjusted her bikini under her jean shorts and blouse. She asked Jarvis, "How far were you planning on going out?"

"Well, not too far. It gets a little dangerous with the tide and the current out past those markers. You know, there are all kinds of killer whales and sharks and stuff out over there in that area!

So we want to play it safe and be cautious," Jarvis explained to Madison.

"Hold on. Forgive me if I see this as ironic, but are you afraid of sharks and a little wind? You sound old! I thought we were going to have some fun. I had planned a romantic secret for you. I might as well leave my bag of surprises in the truck."

"Whoaaaa! Hold up. Maybe we should rethink this. I mean, I checked the forecast, and they said it was a possibility, not a certainty. Let's not be rash and rush to judgment. You can bring the bag. I don't mind going out. I was just trying to think of your well-being. But if you're OK with it, then hey, let's go deep into the ocean."

Jarvis had a cruiser boat that had a pleasure cabin on the inside with a bed, a sink, and a small fridge. It was definitely comfortable seating. They went out into the ocean, and the weather cooperated. When the sun began to set, he decided they had gone out far enough and stopped for a while. He determined now would be a great time to start to rev things up with Madison. She had poured him a glass of wine to go with hers, and she was in her bathing suit at this point. Madison was in a bikini, and her body was amazing. Washboard abs were not usually what most girls strived for, but she literally had no stomach and had abs like a male R&B star on tour; however, she was still incredibly curvy. A perky C-cup-sized black top matched the bottom of her bathing suit. Jarvis was stunned as he caught a glimpse of her in the suit for the first time. He almost stumbled over his words as he looked at her.

"I, um, I sure am glad you brought that bag. Is this for me?" He sat down beside her when he reached out to take the glass. "I am feeling old now. I almost just messed myself looking at you."

Madison crossed her recently waxed legs to seduce him further. "I am hoping you don't mean that because I was ready to open up for you. I mean, we have been seeing each other for a short while now, and I was starting to become comfortable. Actually, I have something else in the bag, but you can't be acting old. For real, you have to be open to trying it. This is supposed to take things to the ultimate level."

"At this point, I believe I am willing to try anything!" JAWS said as he downed his glass and refilled it all the way to the top.

Madison gazed at the sunset as she kicked off her flip-flops. She softly began to rub her feet against his legs. "Don't you want to get more comfortable and take your shoes off?" Jarvis removed his shoes. Madison was now rubbing his feet with hers.

"That is an impressive sunset. The sky is majestic. It is like your loveliness." Jarvis realized he sounded kind of stupid. He still felt uncomfortable around Madison when he spoke to her, it did not feel natural. He had been wanting her for quite some time, but every time he got close to her, he felt something different. He needed to relax. "I don't know why I feel so tense and uneasy."

Madison looked at Jarvis, thinking she may not be able to go through with her plan at this rate. Weird as it was, she kissed him on the cheek to settle him down. "I have something that will make you very relaxed. Are you willing to try these with me?" She handed him four pills.

He took the pills without hesitation and threw them in his mouth.

She asked, "Can we take the boat out a little farther? I am feeling really free, and I don't want anyone to hear or see me."

He jumped up and did as she asked. After about twenty minutes, he came down and said, "I am going to lay down for a little while. Would you like to join me?" As they walked toward the bed, the last thing he remembered was a little music playing.

Jarvis woke up feeling out of it, slightly dazed. However, he could tell the current had begun to rock the boat. He figured it was time to get up and take the boat back closer to shore. As he tried to get out of the bed, he felt a jerk. His left and right wrists were hand-cuffed to the bed, and his feet were tied together unbearably tight.

"Madison!" he yelled.

"I have not gone anywhere," she replied in an abnormal tone as she placed the remaining pieces of the cut-up jump ropes in the bag. "I would not think of leaving you right now. I have been planning this moment carefully for months, and this is years in the making." Her voice clearly filled with rage, but she was not forceful in her speech.

Jarvis noticed that she was not in her bathing suit anymore, but in an all-black wet suit. He started to get uncomfortable with the whole situation and wanted to see if he could get a handle on things.

"I did not know you were into this kind of stuff. I don't re-member much with the pills, but I was planning something sen-sual with you. This looks like you want it rough. What was that you gave me, anyway?"

"This will definitely be rough, alright, and those were just shaved-down Benadryl. I needed you to be asleep. You are heavi-er than I expected. Do you recognize this woman?" Madison held up a picture of Keisha at FAMU on her phone while she played music on it. "What about this song playing?"

"No, I don't recognize her, but if she is on the way, she can get it, too. And gospel music ain't going to stop me from do-ing what I got to do to you. Now, I am all for freaky, but this is getting strange." He tried to make Madison feel a little bizarre, hoping she would begin to turn things to a sexual place. "Do you want to do this or not?"

"Oh, trust me, I am doing this. We are doing this. Are you sure you don't know this woman? You sang this song with her the day you met her." She began to get angry about his ignorance.

"I said no. Who the hell is she to you?"

"No, not is—was! She was my momma. Her name was Keisha Nicole Moore, and she was with you when she was a student at FAMU."

"OK, a lot of women were with me at FAMU. Hold up. What is your whole name?" Jarvis, still clueless but beginning to piece things together, asked.

Madison took a razor blade out of her bag and began cutting Jarvis on his chest and arms so it would not get too messy. "I was named after where my mother met my father, and she gave me a variation of his middle name. I am Madison Alexandria Moore." She backed away from him and watched him grimace with pain as he attempted to make sense of things.

"Are you saying that—that you are my…You are trying to tell me that I am your dad?" He could not believe it. Jarvis thought back, and he could not remember her. He listened to the song playing, which was "I Feel Like Holding On." Then it hit him— but so did Madison.

She punched him hard in the face. Madison was becoming more enraged. "Dad? Bitch what! I ain't saying you my dad! You are barely my sperm donor but you will never be a dad."

"Look, look, I remember her. We met in the financial-aid line, but I had no idea about you. You have to believe me. Please, just let me up. Let's talk about this. We could have a relationship," Jarvis pleaded as Madison had literally knocked some sense into him.

"I don't want a relationship with you. I want you to know the type of pain you inflict on women." She pulled out alcohol to pour on some of his cuts. *SMAAAACK!* She backhanded Jarvis with ferocity after pouring alcohol on three of the wounds she'd inflicted. The other cuts started to bleed, but she made sure not too much, though. She only wanted the blood to cover parts of his chest.

"Please, let me up. Your mom was a beautiful woman, and I really liked her. We just lost touch, and I really did not know about you. She came back to see me once but things got out of hand." Then he recognized it. He never noticed it before now, but he could see so much of his features in Madison. He realized that was why he was so drawn to her, yet so uneasy in her presence.

Madison pulled a gun from her bag. Jarvis was already in fear for his life, but now he knew she was serious. She had lured him out in the middle of the ocean to kill him. He had to fight for his life. He struggled mightily to break free, but the Benadryl had not completely worn off. He did not have his full strength, and Madison was beating him badly.

"I am willing to let you go if you cooperate," she said. "But if you don't follow my commands—and I mean step by step—I will end your life with two in the head."

"OK, I will do anything."

"You better, or you are not going to make it off this boat." She pistol-whipped him.

Jarvis began to bleed profusely from the nose. "What was that for? I am going to cooperate."

Madison took the key from the bag and unlocked Jarvis's left hand free. Immediately, she stepped away from the bed and threw him a rag from the bag. "You can stop some of the bleeding with this."

She continued to give him directions. "Unlock your right hand from the bed and sit up real slow. If you have one false move, I promise you that bed is the last place you will ever lie." Madison cocked back the hammer on the pistol to let him know just how serious she was.

Jarvis did exactly as Madison told him. He was not at full strength and with his feet bound, he felt as if he had no other option. He looked around as he thought of ways to distract her. Thinking about how he could possibly overpower her and take the gun away. With the rag to his nose, he was finally able to stop some of the bleeding. He then turned to the edge of the bed as directed by Madison.

"Now place your feet on the floor and hop toward me and hand me that rag." Madison threw the bloody rag overboard into the shark-infested waters.

Jarvis did not miss one direction. He was terrified at this point, but figured his best chance was to plead for his life. With his hands raised in the air and his feet bound tightly together, he hopped the best he could almost cutting off the circulation. Clumsily taking one little jump at a time. As he continued to think of ways to try get out of this, he reconsidered the previous thought of rushing Madison to get the gun from her because he realized how weak he was from the drugs. He now believed just jumping off to escape would be his best option.

"Is there anything that I can do, Madison? Please spare my life. I know I have not been much of a father to you, but I can try to be now. Just give me a chance."

Madison was angered by Jarvis's petty attempts for sympathy, so she pistol-whipped him twice more in the back of his head. "Mother-fucker you really don't think I will leave you leaking all over this boat, do you? You want to know what you can do? You can give my momma her dignity back!"

Jarvis continued hopping toward the edge of the boat as Madison made him. He turned around when she requested. "What do you want from me? Look in my eyes. Can't you see I really am sorry?"

"No, I can't see anything. But I want you to look in my eyes because death has a face, and it looks a lot like this. I will be the last thing you ever see if you don't hush. Now, if you want a chance to live, you will follow instructions. Back all the way up to the edge of the boat. I only want you to answer the questions I ask you. I have simple questions. You get them right, and you will be OK." Madison's fury was evident in her escalating shouts.

Jarvis was crying at this point. He was a shell of himself, weak and bleeding from his nose and chest. Blood dripped from several parts of his body. Eventually, he pulled himself together because he thought cooperating was the only thing that could save him. "OK, I will answer what you ask and only what you ask. Please just don't take my life, and I can't back up any farther. I am already on the edge."

"OK, I have just one question for you: Are you ready to swim with the shark?" She let off three carefully placed rounds into his legs and shoulder. He fell backward into the rough waters. She made sure she did not end his life but that he would leave a trail of blood in the water.

Reporting Live

*M*adison sprang into action after Jarvis fell. She did not want to take any chances. She took the gloves from her bag and put them on fast. Then she removed the bloodstained sheet and threw it in the waters. At this time, she could see sharks circling the area where her father fell, and she became more flustered. She searched thoroughly and found the shell casings. Once she retrieved all of them, she tossed them overboard. Next, she grabbed the cleaning supplies from her bag and began wiping down the boat wherever she thought she had left fingerprints or any traces of blood. After vigorously cleaning the cabin, Madison sprinted to the top of the boat to take it back closer to the shore. She steered the speedboat about a hundred yards from shore and rested the cruiser. She took all of her belongings and triple-checked the boat to cover her tracks. Then she carefully removed the disposable shoe covers from her shoes, placing them inside the bag before putting it on. Finally, she clicked the timer on her watch and dove in the water.

She made it in enough time according to her wristwatch. She clicked the timer and ran to the red sedan parked by the truck. She removed the keys from her backpack and popped the trunk. Her drenched backpack filled with incriminating evidence needed to be disposed of, so she grabbed the towels from the trunk and dumped the items from the backpack into the towels. She took the larger bag from the trunk, lined it with the other towel, and then placed the backpack and the towels inside of the large bag, looking to limit any water damage. She got in the car and cautiously drove off, trying hard not to peel off or speed so that her exit appeared normal. She checked her watch; the time was 11:15 p.m. "Perfect!" Madison was pleased with her execution so far. After a short while, she began to get paranoid, as she saw lights in the rearview mirror. She tried to calm her nerves and thought lights are normal, everything is fine. She should check for things that were unusual but as she took multiple turns, the lights kept popping up and she was not sure if she had been spotted. She stopped at a small gas station and did not see a car following her so she did not panic. Before exiting, she sat in the backseat and changed out of her clothes into a pair of jeans, a baseball cap, and a T-shirt. She paid the attendant in cash so as not to leave an electronic trail of her whereabouts. After gassing up, she returned the car to Speedy Car Rentals at 11:43 p.m. and put the keys in the drop box. She grabbed the large bag filled with evidence and walked calmly into the night air. As she walked, she reviewed her night; mentally retracing her steps and wondering if she had covered all bases. It took her longer than normal to walk the mile and a half distance; she was careful to observe all that she saw that night. Around 12:30, Madison walked up in her grandmother's driveway; normally it would have taken her about twenty-five minutes but she did not want to appear to be in a rush. However, she did not notice anything strange on the walk home nor did she think anyone had spotted her. She walked in the house, went upstairs, and slept in her mother's old bed.

The next day, her cell phone rang constantly, finally waking her up around noon. Madison looked at the phone's call log. Mr. Clark had been trying to reach her. As she was getting out of bed, he called again.

"Madison, finally. I have been looking to reach you all morning. Are you at your apartment?"

"No, sir, I am back at my grandma's place."

"Well, actually, that is better. I need you to put on work attire and get down to the beach. *This is big*, Madison. This is our shot. I sent a crew down there already. I thought I was going to have to put Lisa on the air, but this is our opportunity. We will definitely be first to the scene."

"What's going on, Uncle Robert?"

"Well, it has yet to be confirmed, but it appears that Jarvis Williams is dead. His assistants have been looking for him since yesterday, and when they could not reach him, they raised hell with the police department. You know it usually takes twenty-four hours for them to start with missing persons. But since it was Jarvis and he has connections with people on the force, they were on the lookout for him. After hours of searching the city without luck, someone spotted his truck and boat out by the ocean. I need you to get there ASAP. The crew should be there in about forty-five minutes. How long will it take for you to get there?"

"I can be ready and there in about an hour."

"You need to be there faster than that, Madison. This is your break. This will be the story of the century here, and I want you to leave your mark all over this. I want WCMG to be there reporting before anyone. Jarvis will make national news, and you could be the face of this story. Get there!"

Madison woke her grandmother with all of the commotion of her getting ready. After showering and getting dressed, Madison heard Mrs. Moore open the door.

"Morning, Maddie," Mrs. Moore said as she hugged her.

"Hey, Big Momma. I am running late for work." She kissed her grandmother as she grabbed her things to go.

Madison drove back to where she had just come from that night. On her way, she had been on the phone with Mr. Clark, receiving instructions on what to do and who to see when she got there. While meeting up with her crew, she watched the police section off areas and the crime-scene investigation team begin forensics work. A detective walked up to her and introduced himself.

"Hi. My name is Alonzo Walker. We cannot have people in this area."

"How are you, Mr. Walker? I am Madison Moore. I believe you spoke with Mr. Robert Clark and told him you wanted us here to cover this so you could get the word out to the community early."

"Oh, OK. You are with Robert's team. I need you all to keep it brief. You can actually tell people he is dead. Ask for people to call this number if they have information." Detective Walker handed her a card with a number on it for anonymous tips.

Madison and the crew set up. As she prepared to go on air, the gravity of the entire situation began to overwhelm her.

Madison's heartrate was ridiculous, her chest pounded in a cartoon-like fashion. She began to shake, and it was obvious. *I have to calm down. It is almost over,* she told herself. Clark Media Solutions was simulcasting her report live from the scene on TV, radio, and on the Internet. The station interrupted all services and went live to the scene. Robert sat in the studio and announced there was breaking news.

"Good afternoon. I am Robert Clark, president and founder of Clark Media Solutions. I am here because of the seriousness of the situation. We interrupt our regularly scheduled programming to bring you breaking news. This is a heartbreaking day for our community, as we have lost an enormous fixture that has become a part of the fabric of FAMU. With more on the story, let's go live to the scene with Madison Moore. Madison, are you there? What can you tell us?"

"Thanks, Robert. Good afternoon, I am Madison Moore. Unfortunately, I am here at the dock near the ocean with the saddening news that iconic Professor Jarvis Alexander Williams has been pronounced dead. He was discovered here sometime this morning. If anyone has any information that they believe could be helpful, you are encouraged to call 850-599-TIPS. Again, that number is 850-599-8477. I am here with Detective Walker. He would like to say a few words. What can you tell us, detective?"

"After several disturbing calls about Mr. Williams, we were placed on alert that he was not able to be reached. Several people close to him believed that despite his frequent travels he would not go somewhere without informing loved ones of his whereabouts. After we placed an alert on his vehicle, it was located out here. We believe that he went out on his boat. After carefully searching the boat, it became apparent that he was involved in something that led to his death. We were in the process of calling divers in when we discovered portions of his body. He has been positively identified by loved ones. We are asking for anyone with information to contact us. Anything you may be able to think of can be helpful. Thank you."

"Thank you, Detective Walker. Again, the news came in early this morning, and it pains me to repeat the great Jarvis Williams, affectionately referred to as JAWS; the iconic Rattler, is deceased. We will have more on this as information rolls in. Back to you, Robert."

Madison and her crew were wrapping up and receiving instructions when the detective's phone began to ring incessantly. As she was about to leave, Detective Walker approached her.

"Ms. Moore, do you mind if I have a few words with you over here?"

"No problem at all."

"How well did you know Mr. Williams?"

"Actually, he was my professor for my final course, and we began to get to know each other on a personal level."

"Is that so? How well did you get to know him personally?" The detective walked Madison back to his vehicle and opened the passenger door for her. They continued the conversation in the front seat of his car.

"Honestly, I sat quietly in the class for most of the semester and did not know him well until a few weeks ago. I saw him out, and he approached me. We exchanged information and began conversing. I would call and text him, and he would call and text me. Occasionally, we would even meet up."

"Is that as far as the relationship went? Did you love Mr. Williams? Did you begin to develop feelings for him after more interactions?"

"I never became intimate with him, Detective Walker. He had sort of a reputation, but I saw him more as a father figure. He always tried to get closer, but he could have been my dad. The crazy thing is he invited me to come out here with him! I had too much to work on, though, and I just could not make it. Maybe I could have…"

Detective Walker was amazed by Madison's candor. Most of the stuff she told him he had received from investigating a tip that had come in. Madison was almost too up-front. He had to be suspicious because the nature of his work just made him that way. Nonetheless, Madison was credible and cool despite appearing emotional. Detective Walker interrupted her and said.

"Do not even say it. You were lucky that you were not here. That could have been both of you out there, and I would have had to investigate what had happened to you as well. Where were you yesterday, if you do not mind me asking?"

"I was not too far from here, at my grandmother's house."

"Do you have her name and information?"

Detective Walker also got Madison's phone number before he exited the vehicle to call Mrs. Moore. Madison went over to the crew to talk to them before they returned to Tallahassee. She was getting into her car when the detective let her know he had spoken with her grandmother.

"Just got off the phone with Mrs. Moore. I feel like I have known her my entire life. She invited me over for dinner, but I have to get back to Tallahassee. I will be in touch if I need to talk with you. I am sorry for your loss. I can't imagine what you must be feeling or thinking at this moment."

Just as she was about to pull out, her phone began buzzing nonstop. She looked at her phone and the notifications and alerts were ridiculous. A memorial page established for Jarvis had her tagged in several posts. Detective Walker's words echoed in her mind. Madison was numb. She felt absolutely nothing, not joy nor sadness. A strange indifference hit her as she drove back to her grandmother's house.

"Maddie Baby, come into the kitchen with me, please," her grandmother said as she entered the door.

"Do I have to Big Momma, I just want to go upstairs and lay down?"

"It will only take a minute, and you can go do that right afterwards." Madison walked in the kitchen to see her grandmother seated at a small table with tears streaming from her eyes and two bowls of ice cream, one for each of them.

"What is this Big Momma?"

"Well this is probably one of your momma's best kept secrets. Strangely enough, she never wrote about this in any of her journals. This was Keisha's favorite ice cream and anytime she did something major, you know accomplish something big this is how we would celebrate. I went by the grocery store to pick it up after I left the church to dump that bag for you. I took G poppa's gun out first. I put that back when I was talking to the detective. Deacon Jones takes all of the stuff we cannot give away on Friday nights down to the landfill and they incinerate it all by the morning. I hope you made that evil bastard suffer!"

Madison could not believe her ears, but she ate her ice cream with her grandmother as they cried and sat quietly.

www.ingramcontent.com/pod-product-compliance
Lightning Source LLC
Chambersburg PA
CBHW071356170626
46811CB00003B/1152